A Hundred Years and a Day

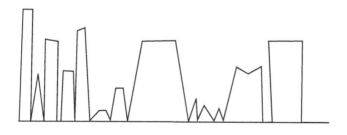

A Hundred Years and a Day

A Hundred Years and a Day

34 stories

Tomoka Shibasaki

translated by Polly Barton

Stone Bridge Press   •   *Berkeley, California*

Published by
Stone Bridge Press
P.O. Box 8208, Berkeley, CA 94707
sbp@stonebridge.com • www.stonebridge.com

The MONKEY imprint was established by Stone Bridge Press in partnership with MONKEY New Writing from Japan.

Cover design by Counterpunch Inc. / Linda Gustafson. Cover image: © Rinjiro Hasegawa.

Hyakunen to ichinichi by Tomoka Shibasaki. Copyright © 2024 Tomoka Shibasaki. All rights reserved. Original Japanese edition published by Chikuma Shobo Ltd. in 2020; revised edition, 2024.

English translation rights throughout the world reserved by Stone Bridge Press, Inc. under the license granted by Chikuma Shobo Ltd.

English translation © 2025 Polly Barton.

First printing 2025.

No part of this book may be reproduced in any form without permission from the publisher.

Printed in the United States of America.

p-ISBN 979-8-9886887-3-0 (paperback)
p-ISBN 979-8-9886887-5-4 (casebound)
e-ISBN 979-8-9886887-4-7 (ebook)

Contents

1

12

One summer during a long rainy spell, student number one from class one and student number one from class two discover mushrooms growing in a flower bed next to a covered walkway at their school; two years after leaving school they bump into each other, but after that, ten years pass, twenty years pass, and they don't meet again

2

20

The tobacco shop on the corner was draped in wisteria that burst into glorious blossom every spring; upon close inspection, it became clear that this wisteria was actually two wisteria plants that had grown intertwined; these days nobody remembered that one of them had been found on the street years before

3

27

A man in exile swims to a bay on an island, where he is rescued by a young boy and an old man; after the war ends, the man stays on in the village but barely speaks to anyone except the young boy

4

34

Daughter Tales I

5

36

Back when there was a fountain in the station concourse, a man known as Hoody would spend all day sitting beside it; one day a woman he'd never met approached him and started yelling at him

6

43
My love for daikon was so great that when I found
myself living in a part of the world where it wasn't
commonly grown, I decided to try growing it myself;
I ended up serving daikon dishes to my neighbors,
and even making up a kids' story about daikon

7

46
The tale of a man who gets off a train at a random stop
and decides to live there, finds a job in a liquor shop in
the nearby shopping arcade, meets a girl at one of the
bars that the liquor store delivers to, and then, after
the girl leaves, moves away to live somewhere else

8

53
Standing outside a small house, three junior high
students who were skipping school look toward
the nearby train station; ten years pass

9

57
Family Tree I

10

59
A ramen shop called House of the Future stayed open
for a long time; the other businesses around it vanished,
apartments were built, and people came and went

11

66
A woman hears an announcement on the radio that war
has broken out; relatives arrive at her house seeking refuge;
when the war ends they leave, then a civil war breaks out

12

73   Ferries that once moored at a certain pier stop running, and for a long time the ferry terminal lies abandoned, but then an affluent investor builds a resort hotel in the area; sometime later a crowd of people watch a new type of aircraft being launched into space from the pier

13

79   All the male children born into a family that ran a public bathhouse were given a name that included a specific kanji character, but nobody knew who first decided that that should be the case

14

88   Daughter Tales II

15

90   Two friends were in the habit of visiting a certain repertory cinema every month; before the screening, they always went to eat ramen, gyoza, and fried rice at a ramen place nearby; once there was someone in one of the movies that they watched who was the spitting image of one of the two friends

16

96   A river whose bank was visible from the second-floor window of a house floods during a typhoon and almost bursts its banks; when the house was first built, there was nothing around it but fields; even further back in the past, there were no people living there

17

102 In a second-hand store unimaginatively called "Second Hand," Abbie finds a book of manga and a novel from Japan; when she shows them to a classmate who can read Japanese, he tells her that the note written on the novel's last page is a love letter

18

109 After two years in a first-floor apartment, the tenant realizes that a certain cat would pass along the street in front at precisely the same time each day; following the cat, the tenant sees it disappear into a vacant house; when the tenant first moved into the apartment, the house wasn't vacant

19

115 I feel like I want to see the places that someone else saw, he said; I like thinking about places I've been to once but I no longer know how to get to, or places that you can only access at certain times, I feel like there must be some way of visiting the places that exist only in people's memories

20

125 Family Tree II

21

128 Mizushima is injured in a traffic accident and is in hospital for a while, but he's left with no permanent physical damage; seven years later, when his memories of the accident are fading, he bumps into Yokota, who had been driving the car that caused the accident, while on a work trip to Tokyo

22

135 A man opens a cafe in a shopping arcade, dreaming that it will become like the jazz cafe he used to frequent as a student; the cafe stays open for nearly thirty years, then closes down

23

142
Growing up, two brothers are often told how close
they are; the older brother moves away to study; the
younger takes up the guitar and becomes famous;
on a TV in an izakaya, the older brother sees his
younger brother for the first time in ages

24

150
Yamamoto found a rooftop apartment to live in, then moved
to another rooftop apartment with a big balcony, then
moved into yet another apartment; at one time there was a
woman around, at another time he spoke with his neighbor

25

157
Daughter Tales III

26

161
In an international airport were some female students
waiting for their flight to begin boarding, a married
couple with a baby, and a woman who had once been
seen off there by her father; before it became an international airport, a man flew a plane from there

27

166
An older sister who's taken a bus to the desert finds
that she has phone reception, so sends a photo
to her younger sister; her younger sister thinks
about the deserts she has visited in the past

28

171
One day, there was a great snowfall in a place where snow
never usually settled; a boy who had run out of his house
saw a black dog in a park, and then immediately afterward
heard someone from his year at school calling his name

29

176   There were several fountains in the underground shopping complex at any one time; a square there known as
Fountain Plaza was used by many as a meeting place;
several decades previously, several years previously,
there had been people waiting for other people there

30

183   Family Tree III

31

185   Mako was always watching TV; after seeing an astronaut on TV she decided to become
an astronaut, and went to the moon

32

188   Back when the first train passed through the area,
my grandmother's grandfather tended a flock
of sheep, and his wife spun their wool; one day,
the two finally began talking to each other

33

196   On the first floor of a building were several small shops; a
woman who opened a cafe at the back of the building was
told by a fortune teller that a bright future awaited her

34

202   At the back of a building that was being demolished
was an apartment that hadn't been touched for decades,
containing a manuscript that someone had left behind;
a man from the demolition company tried to sell
the manuscript but couldn't get any money for it

A Hundred Years and a Day

34 stories

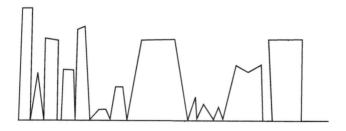

1

One summer during a long rainy spell, student number one from class one and student number one from class two discover mushrooms growing in a flower bed next to a covered walkway at their school; two years after leaving school they bump into each other, but after that, ten years pass, twenty years pass, and they don't meet again

Spotting something unusual in the flower bed, student number one from class one in the first year of high school went over to it and discovered a round white growth.

It's times like these, she thought, that you use the word "unexpected."

Large raindrops struck her vinyl umbrella, making a pattering noise. Student one from class one loved that sound. When it rained, the weed-riddled patches of grass around the flower beds would soak up the rainwater, and when you stepped on the grass it would come oozing out, as if you were walking through swampland.

The mushroom was perfectly white. The grass and the fallen leaves around it were speckled with reddish-brown earth and steeped in muddy water, but not a single fleck of dirt besmirched the mushroom's round white surface. Maybe because it was growing underneath a bush, there were no rain droplets on it either. Student one from class one wondered if someone had brought the mushroom from somewhere else and placed it here. That explanation

12 /

A HUNDRED YEARS AND A DAY / *13*

made more sense to her. Placed it here so that somebody would find it. If that were the case, then she, as the person who had found the mushroom, needed to find out who'd done such a thing.

Student one from class one looked all around her but saw no one. Today she was seriously late. In ten minutes' time, second period would end, and morning recess would begin. They were expected to spend recess in their classrooms for a homeroom meeting.

The flower bed lay next to a covered walkway that connected the gym with the old school building. Student one from class one had entered through the back gate, passing round the back of the gym. From inside, she'd heard shouting. It sounded like a practice match for some kind of ball game.

Student one from class one stepped onto the grass, which was marked "KEEP OFF." The rain seeped out from the ground and the leaves, soaking through her canvas gym shoes in an instant, and a cold sensation spread across her feet.

Crouching down to look, she found another white mushroom positioned further back in the bed than the first one. Then, further back still, another one. The mushrooms were identical in form, but grew progressively smaller. She couldn't see any further than the third, as the ground was obscured by the azalea bush. Student one from class one stepped forward to peer beneath it.

"What're you doing?"

At the sound of this voice from behind her, student one from class one's shoulders tensed up reflexively.

Turning around, she found student one from class two standing there. Student one from class two was holding the exact same kind of transparent vinyl umbrella, on which the raindrops were pattering. The rainfall grew stronger, and the sound grew louder.

Student one from class one was Yōko Aoki, and student one from class two was Yūko Asai. As of last year, their senior high school had started merging the genders in their class registers, but both girls were still unused to their newfound status as "student one." In kindergarten and junior high school, the boys had been listed first in the register, as though that was just the way things were done in the world. Discovering upon entering this school that all that had been no more than convention was well and good, but always having their names read out first and the attention that came with it left them a bit uneasy. The two had spoken about it just once, during gym class.

"There're mushrooms," student one from class one answered. She pointed with her index finger directly at the largest mushroom growing at the front.

"Did you plant them?" student one from class two asked, frowning uncomprehendingly. She seemed to want to ask, why would you do something like that?

"No, no, no. They were just growing here."

"Ah, phew!" student one from class two said, visibly breathing a sigh of relief.

"There was no sign of them yesterday."

"I know! Amazing."

It had been raining for two weeks. It was a cool

A HUNDRED YEARS AND A DAY / *15*

summer, and there'd even been a typhoon, which was rare for July.

Stepping a bit further in and peering closely, they spotted a mushroom that looked exactly like a shiitake. Its size, however, was nothing like that of a shiitake. The cap was at least thirty centimeters in diameter. It was so perfectly shaped that it looked fake. Maybe someone had planted them here, after all.

Just then, something small and blue moved through the corner of the girls' vision.

A small—creature?

The two looked at one another.

"Did you see something?"

"Something whizzing past?"

Patter patter patter, went the rain on their umbrellas. Its rhythm shifted. There's a song that goes like this— what is it again? student one from class one thought, but she couldn't bring it to mind.

The bell rang, and the two girls hurried off to their respective classrooms.

In neither their second nor their third year were they put in the same class, and they left school without ever having much opportunity to speak to one another. Throughout their three years of high school, each of them was always "student one."

In the summer of her second year at university, student one from class one went to see a rock band playing an outdoor concert in Kyoto. The pedestrian crossing in front of the concert venue was teeming with people. As she crossed the road, wiping the sweat dripping from her face while she hurried along in a bid not to lose sight of the friends she'd come with, she thought she heard someone calling her name.

When she reached the other side of the road, she stopped and looked around, and there was student one from class two's face, poking out from the crowd.

"What're you doing?"

"I'm going to the concert."

"Me too."

"You like their music?"

"Hmm, not so much."

Student one from class two laughed. Then both their groups of friends called to them.

"Okay, well, see you around!"

They waved to each other and parted ways. Inside the venue, they didn't see one another again.

Three years later, student one from class one happened to see student one from class two on the TV. The program, screened late at night, was a documentary about one of the remote islands on the Inland Sea. The island had once had a thriving fishing industry, but now its population was declining as more and more people moved away. Among those who did remain, however, there were lots of interesting personalities, and the documentary tracked the various bars, restaurants, and events on the island over the course of a year. There, sitting among the customers of an udon restaurant, was student one from class two. In the evening, she played guitar at the restaurant. The program featured an interview with her. She explained how, after leaving high school, she'd worked a series of part-time jobs, finally arriving six months earlier on the island, where she was helping out at the udon restaurant. She also spoke about a project to convert an empty seafront building into a guesthouse, which would open the following month. The program showed her playing guitar and singing on the beach, too. Student one from class one hadn't known that student one from class two could play the guitar. The song she sang was great. It was a shame that they showed only a short clip.

Student one from class one wanted to speak to student one from class two, but having neither her contact details nor any friends in common, nothing came of it.

The following year, student one from class one moved to Tokyo and started working at a real estate agency. She wrote a film blog that quickly grew popular, and began writing articles for magazines and review sites. Four years after taking up magazine work, she was asked by someone she'd met there to start up a "life advice" feature on late-night radio. They called it "life advice," but the problems featured were nothing too serious, rather the kind of trivial yet slightly niche topics that you'd hesitate to seek advice for elsewhere. The feature had a decent listenership, though, and a good number of people wrote in with their questions. One day, while reading through the messages sent in to the show on social media, she found one that read:

"Ms. Aoki, you're great! I was actually at the same high school as you."

Wondering who the message was from, student one

from class one checked the sender's user account and discovered that, as far as she could work out, it was student one from class two. She hadn't made her real name public, but the account name was a nickname she'd had in high school. It wasn't clear where exactly she was living, but it wasn't the island where student one from class one had seen her on TV ten years earlier. Posted on her account were photos of her with her two children at a shopping mall and a theme park.

Student one from class one contemplated sending student one from class two a message, but the woman in those photos, in which the faces of both the mother and the children had been cleverly obscured, somehow seemed to her a different person from the one she knew, and so she held back. Student one from class two never sent in a direct message, either to student one from class one or to the program. Student one from class one had the feeling that she would run across student one from class two somewhere. Sometime, somewhere, just like when student one from class two had called out to her on the street that summer all those years ago.

The radio feature went on for three years. After quitting the program, student one from class one published three essay collections.

Years later, she was asked by a friend to take up a teaching post at a university. At the end of her first class, one of the students approached her. He was a boy with very pale skin.

"My mom said she went to the same high school as you."

The boy was student one from class two's older son. Their features were similar.

"Is your mom well?"

"She's living in Dalian now. For my stepdad's work."

The boy took out his smartphone and showed her a photo. Student one from class two stood, for some reason wearing a cherry-red sweatsuit, on the deck of a boat moored in a harbor.

"My mom said that you two saw an alien while you were together. A small silver one."

It seemed that student one from class two's son was very eager to hear her tell the story.

2

The tobacco shop on the corner was draped in wisteria that burst into glorious blossom every spring; upon close inspection, it became clear that this wisteria was actually two wisteria plants that had grown intertwined; these days nobody remembered that one of them had been found on the street years before

The tobacco shop on the corner was covered in the most glorious wisteria. In early May, coinciding with the run of public holidays at that time, it would burst into blossom. The long sprays heaving with tiny purple flowers that cascaded from its wall brightened the whole block.

The wooden door to the tobacco shop was now kept shut, but it had at one time stood open. When the apartment building opposite was first built, the vending machines outside the shop were still working, and there'd been a person sitting at the kiosk window alongside them.

Even further back in time, when there were still lots of fields in the area, and the smell of boiling soybeans from the nearby tofu shop began wafting into the air before the sun was up, a young girl would emerge from the tobacco shop and make her way to elementary school. She always met with three of her classmates on the next corner. So scared were they of being barked at by the big Kai Ken that lived in a house along the way that they would frequently take a detour. The dog was kept inside the gate, but sometimes it would stand up and rest its front paws on the railings. This terrified the girls, who thought it might leap out at any second. Around the time the girl left the school, the dog disappeared. For about six months before that, it had spent its days lying stretched out by the door to the house. Even then, it would raise its head and bark at the girls whenever they passed. The girl remembered that for a long time after.

Back when the girl was born, the wisteria—which had been transplanted into a plastic barrel used for pickling—had begun to climb the wall, just about brushing the side of the shop's awning. At that time, most customers bought their cigarettes from the kiosk window positioned above the glass case, rather than from the vending machines. The shop also stocked a selection of other items: weekly magazines, candy, cleaning products, and so on. For a spell, there was a row of stools in there too, for the local kids to sit on while they ate their candy inside the shop. A little boy living in the apartment building in front of the bus stop came in almost every day. His father wasn't around, and his mother, who was bringing him up alone, had to go out to work.

The boy's mother was a distant relative of the woman who was always sitting at the kiosk window, which was why the mother had told her son that if she was kept late at work and he had nowhere to go, then he was to stay inside the tobacco shop. The woman in the shop would attempt to make conversation with the boy, asking him if he had any homework, or what he'd had for lunch that day, but he hardly responded, just read his manga. When the boy entered fifth grade, his mother got sick and the boy moved away, having been taken in by one of his relatives. On the boy's final visit to the tobacco shop, he noticed a puppy that looked like a black baby bear, tied to a leash outside a house that lay along his route.

The tobacco shop had been built by the woman's husband's father. As a young man he'd been a carpenter, and even afterward, had often helped out on construction sites. The house he'd lived in previously he'd also built himself.

One day, about a year after the building was completed, the husband's father came to visit. He lived twenty minutes away by tram, and the tobacco shop lay between his house and his workplace, so he was in the habit of stopping by every week or so, but unusually, that particular day he came on a Sunday morning. He brought with him a plant, which, he said, had been left behind by someone who'd moved out of his neighborhood. It was a wisteria, he said, but it being winter, the plant had neither flowers nor leaves, just a splay of frail-looking branches. It was hard to imagine a plant like this ever bearing ornate purple clusters of flowers like those that dangled from traditional hairpins. As father and son drank together, they discussed how they could maybe grow the wisteria so that it hung down from the eaves of the building, since the lack of a garden meant constructing a pergola was out of the question. At any rate, though, the day when that might be accomplished seemed a long time off. The man's wife was still young at this point.

They'd inherited the business from relatives who

A HUNDRED YEARS AND A DAY / *23*

lived very close by. It was the man's wife who ran the shop, and, later on, also his daughter.

One hot summer's day, a man buying a pack of American cigarettes inquired,

"Do you know anyone by the name of Kuramoto living around here?" He was a tall middle-aged man wearing a white shirt and a straw hat.

"Hmm, I don't think so. Do you?"

The wife turned around to consult her daughter sitting further inside the shop. The daughter shook her head.

"They were very good to me, a long time ago. I'm pretty sure their house is around here, but I can't seem to find it."

The man explained that the house in question was a grand sort of residence, with pine trees growing by the gates. The two women couldn't think of where he might mean.

"They say that this area has changed a lot. The tofu shop next door has been here longer than us, so they might know."

The locals often discussed how, until ten years previously, this area had been fields. There'd been a poultry farm, too. The land on which the tobacco shop was built had previously grown green vegetables.

The man looked around him, dissatisfied, then noticed the wisteria that had grown so as to partially cover the shop's awning. It was summer, and its lime-green leaves were bursting forth with great energy.

"Ahh, what a wonderful wisteria! I'd love to see it when it's in flower."

24 / TOMOKA SHIBASAKI

"It's nice, isn't it? We barely do a thing to it, but when it blooms it looks a little like a noren curtain hanging down."

"I can imagine. Gosh, I'm envious. I live in a housing complex, and I've only got a small balcony."

After heaping praise on the wisteria, the man bought some stamps, which he seemed to have just remembered he needed.

"This wisteria is going to have the most incredible flowers one day, I'm sure of it," he said before he went off.

Later on, the wife from the tobacco shop asked the people from the tofu shop next door if they knew of a house in the neighborhood owned by someone called Kuramoto. The tofu-shop owner said that the Kuramotos used to live on the block behind, where two apartment buildings now stood. They'd been a family of some importance, but the business had faltered, they'd run up huge debts, and then vanished entirely. That man with the straw hat stopped in here too, but he seemed suspicious—he was a detective, no doubt about it, the tofu shop owner said, with total conviction.

One morning about a week later, when the husband stepped out of the house to go to work, he found a potted plant sitting outside the tobacco shop. Its leaves looked the same as those of the wisteria that stretched up to the awning. It could hardly have been left there by accident, but there was something unsettling about it being there, so for a while they left it where it was. Yet nobody came to collect it, and none of the neighbors had spotted anybody leaving it there, either. At some point, the wife from the tobacco shop began watering it when she watered her own wisteria, and the following year, it flowered. The flowers were the exact same hue as those of their own wisteria. Both the wife and the daughter thought of that man in the straw hat, but he hadn't been back since that first visit. The second wisteria grew steadily, and at some point, it became impossible to tell which part of the foliage belonged to which plant.

The daughter got married at twenty-six and moved to a nearby town. The husband gave up his construction job at retirement age, and died ten years later. The wife continued to run the shop by herself. All day, she sat at the window by the glass-fronted case full of cigarettes. There was a small TV next to her that was always on, regardless of whether she was watching it. The door to the shop was now closed, and instead, there was a row of three vending machines.

The man with the office job who lived in the house round the corner remembered that scene very well. When he first moved to the house, he hadn't yet quit smoking. As a rule he bought his cigarettes from the convenience store in front of the station, but on occasion, he would buy them at the tobacco shop. In the space of time between pressing the button on the vending machine and retrieving his packet from the compartment, he would glance at the old woman sitting inside. He remembered that she was always looking off to one side, but he couldn't recall her face. He could clearly hear the voice of the TV announcer, reading the news.

The wisteria was only in flower for a short while.

One day, as he approached the shop, the man was thinking to himself that it must be about time for the wisteria to bloom—and then found himself confronted by a curtain of lilac. He was rushing to work at the time, so he thought to himself that he'd come back on Saturday to take a photo, but by then the flowers had already faded. During winter, when the plant was stripped of leaves, he would forget that there was a beautiful wisteria there at all.

One year, some of the flowers that had previously been purple bloomed a bright white. Several of these bright-white clusters hung down from the plant, visible even from a distance. People passing by would wonder to themselves, had those always been here?

The following May, both the tobacco shop and the wisteria had disappeared from the corner.

3

A man in exile swims to a bay on an island, where he is rescued by a young boy and an old man; after the war ends, the man stays on in the village but barely speaks to anyone except the young boy

As the war was coming to an end, a man hid himself on an island. He had fled from a place that lay beyond the mountains rising from the opposite shore.

The man didn't believe that the war was about to end. Nobody believed it. They thought that it would go on at least for another few years. That was why the man had escaped, swum across the sea, and taken shelter on the island. Swimming was the only thing that he was really good at.

Within less than a month, the war had ended. For a while, the man didn't realize that this was the case. He had hidden himself in a cave beneath an outcrop of trees, in the skirts of a mountain that stood inland from a bay. It was summer, so the trees, grasses, and vines were all growing luxuriantly, sheltering the cave from view of the little village in the bay.

When the night plunged both the mountain and the village into darkness, the man would emerge from the cave to steal vegetables from the fields, and to catch shellfish and sometimes fish from the rocky beach. He attempted to use the vegetables he'd stolen to grow his own in the soil of the mountain, but his attempts weren't met with much success. Once he ate the purple fruit hanging from the trees, and came down with a fever and a bad stomach. For three days, he lay curled up on the cold, hard rock of the cave, groaning in pain and wondering whether this would be how he died. Which was better: dying like this, or on the battlefield? Surely this had to be better than sustaining a terrible injury, or getting your body blown to shreds by a bomb? Better, too, than killing numerous people. Or maybe he wouldn't have made it as far as the battlefield—maybe he would have starved to death while walking through the mud, carrying objects which bore no relation to him and which may or may not have been of any use to anyone. He'd seen several people die after being attacked by their senior officers or contracting infectious diseases. This was better than that, surely? He would die here unnoticed, and then, in a few days, wild dogs or some such would eat his corpse. Or maybe he didn't have enough flesh left on him, and what little there was would taste too disgusting to be of interest even to animals.

The man didn't know how much time had elapsed, but he opened his eyes to find his stomach pain gone. His fever, too, had passed. Dragging his impossibly lethargic body as best he could, he crawled out of the cave, but there his energy ran out, and he lay unmoving. After a while, he became aware of someone approaching.

It was a skinny boy who couldn't have been ten years old. The boy stared down intently at the man. Having ascertained that the man couldn't really move—in other words, that he was unable to inflict harm—the boy said something.

A HUNDRED YEARS AND A DAY / *29*

The man understood half of the words that came out of the boy's mouth. He knew that the boy was asking him if he was going to die, or if he could still live. I don't know, the man replied. In truth, he wasn't really sure if he was alive or already dead. He felt as though he had died a long time ago, and what was happening now was a kind of dream.

The boy continued to gaze down at the man for a while, then tossed one of the pebbles lying at his feet in his direction. The pebble landed near the man's arm, but the man didn't react in any way. The boy said nothing, turned on his heels, and disappeared into the bushes.

After two more days, the man could get up. Subsisting on water, he sat propped up against the wall of the cave. He could hear the high-pitched cries of birds echoing through the forest but saw no sign of them. Mice or some other kind of small brown creature would go scuttling past the cave, but he had no means of catching them. As he looked in the direction that one of these creatures had run off, the boy appeared again. Behind him stood an old man. The two approached and said something. The man couldn't understand a word that the old man was saying. The old man was about as skinny as the man himself and had no hair or eyebrows.

The old man held out something that looked like a round dumpling, yellowish in color. The man crammed it into his mouth. It didn't taste of anything. The only thing that lingered in his mouth was an unpleasant stickiness.

The boy said something that the man understood as an instruction to follow them. Gathering all his strength, the man descended the mountain. The village people watched him from afar.

The old man lived in what appeared to be a fisherman's hut, near the water. A harpoon, a net, and other fishing equipment lay strewn across the dirt floor. An old woman, whom he took to be the old man's wife, sat inside. The old woman could speak the man's language. That was how he discovered that the war was over. Their son had died, she told him, so the man could work in his place. The man nodded. He didn't have any other ideas for what to do.

The man had grown up by the seaside, and he adjusted to the way of life there surprisingly quickly. At dawn he would head out to sea in a small boat to catch fish, and during the day, he tended a small field at the base of the mountain. The village people were never aggressive toward him, but they didn't speak to him either. They watched him from a distance, and no visitors came to the house where he was staying.

The only person he conversed with sporadically was the boy, the first person he'd met from the village. The boy had come to live with distant relatives here in the bay after his parents in a far-off town had become embroiled in the war and died. The boy was better at catching fish than anyone. He could dive into the sea and spear even sizable fish with a harpoon. Sometimes he would share his catch with the man.

After finishing junior high school, the boy left the bay. He had never really felt at home in his relatives' house, or with the people in the village. On the day the

A HUNDRED YEARS AND A DAY / *31*

boy departed, the man crossed over the mountain to the port in the next bay to see him off. Thank you, the boy said. The man repeated the same words. On the boat that pulled into the port were ten children about the same age as the boy.

Some time later, the old man who had rescued the man died. That was how the man discovered that he had been the oldest person in the village. The man began to take care of the old woman, who could no longer walk. The old woman told him that she'd been born in a place close to his hometown. She'd left with her mother when she was five and hadn't been back since. Her mother had told her she should never return, she said. The old woman had been separated from her mother at the age of ten, and not long after, came to this village in the bay. If you ever go back there, I want you to visit the place where I was born, the old woman said to the man.

When the old woman died, the man burned down the house where they'd been living and crossed the sea in a boat that he'd built himself. It was the first time he'd left the island since swimming over that long-ago summer.

The peninsula across the water had changed a lot. Big factories had been built by the port, and trucks made their way back and forth across a newly constructed bridge. The man set out walking. He walked for a week until he came to a big city. He spent ten years in the city, working as a day laborer. When he'd finally saved up a little money, he set out for the port again and got on a large ship headed for his hometown. As the ship pulled away from shore, he was struck by the unshakeable feeling that there was someone he knew among the big crowd of people who had come to the wharf to see the ship off. There was no way that could be, but still he stared at the sea of faces as they grew smaller and smaller.

The man's destination was not the seaside town where he was from, but the small village in the valley where the old woman was born. The man walked away from the main stretch of the village, as the old woman had instructed him, and headed along the river beside the fields that lay staggered up the slope. He didn't see any houses, but he did find a large tree. Its shape was just as the old woman had described. The man sat down by its roots and looked out for a long time at the village beyond the fields. A local couple walking past noticed him sitting there.

The only time the boy returned to the bay was thirty years after the man saw him off the island. The population had shrunk considerably by then, and he noticed a number of abandoned houses. Everyone living in the village was old. The boy's relatives with whom he'd been staying back then had already left.

The boy went down to the beach and looked for the house where the man had lived, but found no trace of it. Turning back toward the sound of the waves, he found the sea reflecting the sun, bright and blue. He went up to the water's edge, where he saw small fish swimming in the clear water.

As he was dipping his feet in that familiar sea, a middle-aged couple appeared, cameras round their necks. He looked at them, surprised to find tourists in a place like this, and the couple began speaking to him. My relatives used to live here, and I came here once before a long time ago, when I was a child, the man said. Which house was theirs, the man who was formerly the boy asked, but the man couldn't remember. They asked him to take a picture of the two of them. With pleasure, the man who was formerly the boy replied, and took the camera.

He pointed the camera at the couple standing together on the seashore bright with the sun's glare. Suddenly, as he was positioning them within the frame, a vivid memory came back to him, of grilling and eating the fish that he'd caught with the man, right in that very spot.

"You're incredible," he remembered the man telling him, and how happy he'd been.

4

Daughter Tales I

There was a weirdo in the first company I worked in, the daughter said. He talked to himself all the time, and to the machinery as well. He'd be there in front of the photocopier or the shredder or the coffee machine or whatever, saying, what are you doing, stop messing around, you understand what I'm asking you, don't you? I'd hear him chattering away constantly, the whole time I was in the office.

Then one day, I saw him on the train home. I knew that wasn't the train line that he took to get home, that he lived on another line. He got off at the same station as me, though, so I ended up following him, and I saw him disappear inside a cooking school. I remembered then that he brought in his own lunch every day. I waited around for a while, but he didn't come out, so in the end I went home. The next day, he said to a brand-new model of photocopier that had just arrived in the office, I know it's our first time meeting and everything, but you don't need to be shy with me. He was very good at his job, though, and interacted totally normally with all the people in the office.

Then, at the next place I worked, there was another weirdo. I know I found him really, really weird, but I've forgotten now in what way. That happens sometimes, doesn't it?

34 /

The mother, who was listening, had only two years' experience working in an office, and even that was just a small graphic design company set up by someone who'd been in the grade above her at school. She tried to imagine how it would feel to spend most of the day in the same room as oddballs like that, and other people who you didn't know very well, but she couldn't really picture it.

The daughter's tales went on. At the place where she was working now, there was a dog. The company president had got it from one of her relatives, thinking it would have a soothing effect on the company employees. At first it was just a puppy, but now it's bigger than me, the daughter said. But I've known it since it was a puppy, so it still looks like a puppy to me. Its expression hasn't changed, and its mannerisms or whatever are exactly the same, she said earnestly.

5

Back when there was a fountain in the station concourse, a man known as Hoody would spend all day sitting beside it; one day a woman he'd never met approached him and started yelling at him

This story takes place back when there was still a fountain in the station concourse.

The fountain had a round tray-like object in its center where the water came out, surrounded by a circular pool. The rim of the fountain was made of black stone, and there would always be people sitting on it as they waited for whomever they were supposed to be meeting. The bottom of the pool was strewn with coins people had tossed in, shining darkly beneath the surface of the water, which rippled and glinted under the station's fluorescent lights.

It wasn't unusual back then for the man to spend all day beside the fountain. On the days when he had no work, which was to say most days, he tended to be close by. Occasionally he'd be moved on by a security guard or someone on staff, but back then they weren't as heavy-handed as they are now, and mostly they let him be. The man wore a green windbreaker, and when he stepped outside the station he'd put the hood up, so people knew him as Hoody. The men who called him Hoody had no steady job or place to stay, and slept in the vicinity of the station, like Hoody himself.

The economic climate was considerably better back then, and even those living in stations or on the street could find work as day laborers. The wages weren't at all bad, either. Hoody saved up the money he earned and kept it, together with his possessions, in a coin locker in the station. He planned to leave the city and rent a place of his own when he'd saved enough.

Half a year went by with Hoody hanging around by the fountain. At one point, a brawny guy who'd drifted in from somewhere or other began picking on him. He kicked Hoody while Hoody was sleeping under the footbridge, and messed up his things, so for a while Hoody had to avoid the station, but eventually the man was picked up by the police, and Hoody returned.

One evening, Hoody was perched on the edge of the fountain, lost in thought. It was early winter, and it looked cold outside. The station building kept out the wind, and during the evening rush, the sheer number of people passing through was enough to steam up the concourse.

Hoody's eyes traced the huge crowds of people streaming up to the ticket gates and then pouring out of them, the people cutting across the concourse to change lines, descending into the subway or crossing the footbridge, being absorbed into the bustle of the city that stretched beyond the station complex. He took in the endless flow of people, who appeared only to disappear soon after. He didn't focus on any particular individual, simply let them drift en masse through his vision. He found that after a while people's faces began to fade, that they came to seem like hordes of noppera-bō, faceless spirits gliding by. The sound of their footsteps eddied around him, like the noise of the waves or wind.

"How's tricks?"

The person who addressed him was a slight man, a bit older, who everybody called Carp on account of the Hiroshima Carp baseball cap he wore. Carp settled down beside Hoody.

"Ah, you know," Hoody said, glancing up at Carp's wrinkled face, cast in shadow by the peak of his baseball cap. "Same old."

As he spoke, Hoody continued to watch the tide of people before him, and Carp followed his gaze, trying in vain to see what he was looking at.

"Anything going on?" Carp took a short cigarette out of his pocket. In those days, smoking was permitted even there on the concourse, but Carp didn't light the cigarette, just rolled it between the fingers of his right hand.

Unsure of how to reply, Hoody's gaze alighted on the woman leaning against the column in front of him. She wore a plain gray suit, and was glaring at the clock above the fountain, presumably waiting for someone who hadn't shown up. She looked a lot like his fifth-grade teacher, he thought.

"I was just thinking, someone I know back from elementary school once told me he worked around here."

Hoody said this just for something to say, but once the words were out of his mouth, he had the feeling that someone had actually told him something of the sort, though he had no idea who it was, or when.

Carp laughed through his nose. "Well, that figures. This

is the busiest part of town. There's people doing all sorts here—shopping, eating, visiting love hotels, the whole kit and caboodle."

Carp had a loud voice, and a young man sitting nearby, most likely a student, turned to look in their direction. The black frames of his glasses were held together with tape. Their gazes met, and the young man quickly looked away. The woman in the gray suit had moved away from the pillar and was walking toward the ticket gates, having evidently given up on the person was she was waiting for.

"I guess so."

Once again, Hoody's eyes roved around the space in front of him. There were so many people, it was impossible to know who to look at. The dusty air hit the back of his nose.

"Even if he does work here, I guess he wouldn't recognize me now."

"I was super popular with the girls when I was a student," said Carp. "Had 'em fighting over me and everything—it was pretty wild." Apropos of nothing, Carp went on to tell Hoody how there'd been a terrible scene between some girl who insisted on coming around to his boarding house every day to make him dinner and his girlfriend from back home.

"Somehow I can see that. That you'd be popular when you were young, I mean."

"Really? What makes you think that? C'mon, let's hear it."

"Hmm, you're, um ... You're a smooth talker?"

"Ach, that's a half-assed answer."

"Is it?"

"Hey!"

A different voice burst in over their conversation. In front of Hoody stood a woman in a white coat. She had a side part and wore pale-blue eyeshadow and bright-red lipstick. It was a look shared by many women at that time.

"What the hell are you doing here?" The woman looked just over thirty.

"I'm just ... I'm just sitting."

Paying no mind to Hoody's obvious confusion, the woman carried on, furious.

"Why are you giving me that look? Don't tell me you've forgotten who I am? I thought you were serious about me, after you said you'd take me to your house in Wakayama!"

"I do have a grandma who lives in Wakayama, but ..."

"So you were just stringing me along! What an idiot I was, thinking you'd actually be in touch."

"Can I ask how you know me?"

"Oh, this is too much! Kurata! Class nine, year three at Nishi High. I sat next to you, remember?"

"Kurata ... ?"

"YŪKO KURATA! Imagine forgetting my name! What a cold-hearted man you are! Aren't I right?" The woman looked to Carp for agreement.

"He can be a bit dim at times, this one."

"A bit!? I waited for you, all that time. But I see now that I was a fool!" With that, the woman stormed off into the crowd and disappeared.

"Well, well! A real looker! I can see you don't do too badly with women yourself!" Carp said, with a smirk.

"I've honestly never seen her before in my life," Hoody said. "I went to an all-boys' high school."

"Huh? Well, who was she then?"

"She must've mistaken me for someone else."

"I guess there's no shortage of strange folk in this world." Carp finally brought the cigarette to his lips.

Three months later, Hoody rented an apartment with the money he'd saved and began working for a construction company. Carp disappeared before then. Nobody knew where he'd gone. It was the norm among those who congregated by the fountain for nobody to know anything about anybody else.

Thirty years went by, and Hoody rarely recalled that he'd ever been known as "Hoody." He lived in another prefecture. He didn't have a family, but he wasn't out of work, and he got by.

For the first time in several years, Hoody returned to the station where he'd once spent so much time. He was there to board a high-speed train. The fountain had vanished a long time ago. The station had been renovated, and the concourse had been relocated.

After traveling for an hour, Hoody got off the high-speed train at a station near a large lake. There were apartment buildings in front of the station, and it looked altogether different from when Hoody had left. His sister had been in touch after a decade to tell him that the house they'd once lived in was going to be demolished, and he'd decided to go see it before it was gone.

After a twenty-minute stroll, he arrived at the old house near the river.

The demolition was already underway. The house was cloaked in a white sheet. With half of the building already gone, broken columns, beams, and the insides of rooms were exposed to the open air. Moving closer, peeping through the cracks in the sheet, Hoody saw a coin trapped beneath a cracked tile on the ground. The coin was small and bright silver—he couldn't tell if it was a toy or some kind of commemorative souvenir.

For some reason, Hoody found himself thinking of the fountain, and the coins that lay there at the bottom of the water. He'd stared at those coins for hours on end. He'd spent entire days by that fountain, and not once had he seen anybody toss in a coin.

6

My love for daikon was so great that when I found myself living in a part of the world where it wasn't commonly grown, I decided to try growing it myself; I ended up serving daikon dishes to my neighbors, and even making up a kids' story about daikon

My grandmother harvested a meter-long daikon from her field. First the woman living next door came over to help her pull it out, and then our relatives living in the house behind hers.

My grandmother had grown unusually large vegetables before, not to mention weirdly shaped ones—those with numerous fingers, or twisted like lengths of rope. Each time she dug one up, she'd take a photo and send it to my mother. She never sent us any of the vegetables, though, saying that it would be a waste if they got damaged in transit.

It took an entire day to unearth the daikon, which stretched to over a meter long. Even more than my grandmother, it was the next-door neighbor who was steadfast in her conviction that they mustn't damage the thing, insisting that they scoop out the soil with their hands. It was cold out, but the further down they dug, the warmer it got. That must be how it managed to grow so long, one of the younger relatives had said. You would think, if that were true, it would have meant that other daikon from that field would also be large, but the rest were

/ 43

normal size. Still, when the young man said that, everyone nodded.

While excavating the daikon, those assembled in the field discussed excitedly how it should be eaten. The conclusion of their extensive discussion was that the head should be simmered, the middle shredded to make oroshi, and the tail pickled to make takuan.

All of this I heard from my mother, by letter.

Where I live, on the other side of the Pacific, they don't sell daikon. The closest are the little balls like round candies that they call "radishes," which in Japanese we call "twenty-day daikon."

It was only when I noticed, on my third day here, that there weren't any daikon for sale anywhere, that it occurred to me for the first time that maybe the people living in this country don't eat it.

There were no daikon in the little supermarket in the middle of town, none in the place close by selling organic food, and none in the big supermarket fifteen minutes' drive away. I never saw daikon being sold in the farmers' market held in the square outside the church on Sunday, either.

So I tracked down some mail-order daikon seeds and decided to start growing them in my spare time, when I wasn't working as a teacher. Fortunately, there was space for a vegetable patch in the garden of the place I was renting. I prepared the earth, fertilized the soil, and planted the seeds just as instructed in the advice I'd read online, but the daikon only grew to a length of twenty centimeters or so. I couldn't figure out whether it was the soil or the climate that was to blame.

Each year from then on, I would try doing something a bit different. In the winter of my seventh year, I finally managed to grow daikon the size they were in my head. I used them to make various daikon dishes for the people living near me: braised daikon with a miso sauce, oden, daikon simmered with pork, daikon oroshi, daikon salad. The dishes went down well, and I even gave some daikon cooking classes at my home to local foodies.

After a while, a popular cafe in the area began serving daikon salad. Five years later, the cafe's sliced daikon and ham sandwich became one of its signature dishes.

Yet what I really wanted to eat, more than anything, was takuan: yellow pickled daikon. Every time I thought about its distinctive crunch and smell, I would feel a burst of nostalgia. I tried stringing up the daikon I'd grown to dry under the eaves of my house to make takuan. Yet maybe owing to the rainy climate, my experiment didn't go well, and even after ten years of attempts, I'd not succeeded in making decent takuan.

I wrote a story about all of this, where I imagined a world where the place I lived, White Valley, had been named after all of the daikon growing there. I was initially planning to make it into a picture book, but I was so busy growing the daikon and giving cooking classes in my spare time that nothing ever came of it.

Nothing grows in my grandmother's field now. The kids from our relatives' house behind hers use it to play soccer.

7

**The tale of a man who gets off a train at a random stop
and decides to live there, finds a job in a liquor shop in
the nearby shopping arcade, meets a girl at one of the
bars that the liquor store delivers to, and then, after
the girl leaves, moves away to live somewhere else**

On his way home from visiting a friend who'd moved to
a far-off part of the city, Katō decided to take a different
train line than the one he'd used to get there. The station
closest to his friend's place was served by lines operated
by two different rail companies: one running from north
to south, and one running from west to east.

Katō boarded a westbound train. Past the seventh
station the train moved underground and, without any
scenery to gaze at out the window, Katō felt bored, so he
got off at the next station. A lot of people got off with him.

The station had seven exits, so he took exit number
five, which was his favorite number. Just in front of the
exit was the entrance to a shopping arcade. The arch-
shaped sign for the arcade read "Something or Other
Ginza." It was a name he felt he'd heard before. Maybe he'd
read it in a book a long time ago.

The shopping arcade appeared to have been there for
ages. The speakers attached to the lampposts were blasting out hit songs from the good old days, and gaudy plastic flowers hung down in sprays. In the midday heat, there
were few people around for how many shops there were.

A HUNDRED YEARS AND A DAY / *47*

Katō wandered through the shopping arcade. When he happened upon the type of shop you could go in and come out again empty handed, like a second-hand bookstore, a supermarket, or a shop selling cheap clothing, he'd enter and leave without buying anything. The shop owners and clerks looked as though they had a lot of time on their hands.

At the end of the arcade was a real estate office. There were pieces of paper showing floor plans plastered across the windows and door, so that he could barely see inside. Pushing open the door, Katō found himself immediately confronted by a man at a desk positioned right in front of him. It was an extremely small office.

"Looking for a place to rent?" the man behind the desk said, in a not very friendly tone. This was probably down to the fact that, in the holey T-shirt he'd borrowed from his friend and the jeans he hadn't washed in a good while, together with the plastic supermarket bag he was carrying, Katō didn't look like a person with much money.

"Mmm, yeah," Katō replied.

"It's quite expensive around here, you know."

The man looked up at Katō, as if inspecting him.

"Mmm, yeah," Katō said.

"But you're in luck, actually, because I've got a real find for you. It's not big, but it's very reasonably priced."

The real estate agent led Katō to the apartment directly behind the office. It was an oldish two-story building. The paint on the steep staircase was peeling off in what looked like scales. It was the last apartment on the second floor: a single room of 7.5 square meters with no balcony, but it overlooked the graveyard at the back of the temple, and got a reasonable amount of light.

"With a graveyard there's no risk there'll be anything built there in the future, the air quality's good, and it's safe," the estate agent explained.

"Mmm, yeah," Katō said. He decided to take the apartment. It was his first move from the part of town where he'd lived all his life. Not long after he made this move, his friend, who had lived eight stations away, returned to the place where they'd both grown up.

Katō found a job in a liquor shop in the arcade. His main tasks were doing deliveries and organizing the storeroom. He delivered to the pubs and bars inside the arcade and near the station. Most of the time when he did his deliveries, the places were not yet open, and the kids working there part-time came out to receive the stuff. Katō worked just four days a week, and the rest of the time he read books from the second-hand bookshop, which he sold back to the shop once he'd read them, drinking cheap booze in his room while staring out the window at the trees in the graveyard.

In time, he began chatting with a girl who worked part-time in one of the bars he delivered to. Her name was Satō. She was studying at a nearby university, working at the bar to save money for tuition, but at some point she had to start sending money back home as well, and she ended up quitting her studies.

Satō lived two stations away, so sometimes, when she finished work in the small hours, she would stay at Katō's flat. The first time she visited him and saw the graveyard, she let out an exaggerated squeal. It looks exactly like the graveyard back home, where we used to play dare, she told him excitedly. One of her classmates had toppled a gravestone on a dare, and for a while after, kids at the school kept reporting that they'd seen a ghost. The boy who had toppled the gravestone moved to another school and then died in an accident, Satō related as though it were the punchline to a funny story. "I mean with something that predictable you have to laugh, don't you," she said sitting down by the window that looked out across the graveyard.

One day, after they'd been seeing each other for about six months, Katō went to Satō's bar for a delivery and Satō informed him, with all the casualness of a perfectly regular greeting, that she was getting married to someone else and moving to Okinawa. When he went on his delivery round the following day, she was no longer there.

Katō began seeing another girl working in the same bar, but just around the time he was starting to feel fed up with the arcade, his bike got stolen, and so he decided to take it as a sign and move on. The furniture he owned amounted to a single folding table, and he had only two bags' worth of possessions.

Gazing at the map at the train station, Katō found the name of the place where Satō had lived as a child, and decided to go there. For a full hour, the scenery that passed in front of the window was an unbroken stretch of flat land. There were rice paddies and fields, patches of abandoned land and woods, and a sprinkling of two-story houses and apartment buildings. It was the first time Katō had seen such a long tract of scenery unpunctuated by any hills or mountains.

50 / TOMOKA SHIBASAKI

Finally, though, a small mountain appeared, at whose foot lay the station of the town where Satō had once lived. It seemed like the town's population had shrunk significantly from what it had once been. Aside from a single convenience store, all the shops outside the station had their shutters down. Walking up a gentle slope, Katō found a temple. He took a look inside, but it didn't seem to have a graveyard. There was a pond, with black koi swimming around. He was crouching down to see them better when an old man started up a conversation with him. It turned out that the old man's dog had gone missing. Katō walked around the area with him looking for it, but they didn't find it.

Speaking with the old man, Katō discovered that his relatives' house had been vacant for a while and was falling into disrepair as a result, so Katō decided to move in. It was a single-story building, a bit like a warehouse. There were a couple of leaks, but otherwise it was in better condition than he'd imagined, and after some minor repairs, the water worked fine. Katō took a job at the convenience store in front of the station. It was a small town, and within a month he knew the faces of almost all of the customers. Among them was the head priest at the temple in the next town along. When Katō asked if the temple there had a graveyard, the priest replied that it did. He asked whether one of the gravestones had been toppled by a elementary school child about fifteen years ago, as a dare, and the priest said that he was pretty sure that yes, such a thing had happened, so Katō decided to go and visit on his next day off.

It was a hot, sunny day. When he arrived at the

A HUNDRED YEARS AND A DAY / *51*

graveyard on his bike, he found that it was quite large. In what Katō could only assume was part of some kind of regional trend, all of the gravestones were made of shiny black stone. It felt utterly different from the graveyard next to his previous apartment. He asked the head priest to show him the grave whose stone the kid had toppled. They had fixed the chipped section at the end of the stone, though, so it looked even newer and grander than the other gravestones. The boy who had toppled it was related to the priest, Katō found out. He had grown up playing in the graveyard, so he would often bring his friends here and dare them to do things. Now he was studying in the UK, the priest said. Most likely, he wouldn't ever return to the countryside here.

After staying on for a year at the convenience store, Katō began working for a local construction company. The owner of the company was a customer at the convenience store. His son, who he had always assumed would take over the business, had run away from home and not been in touch for some time, and the owner was debating whether or not to close the company, which had just four employees. The company sponsored Katō in getting his license for driving trucks and heavy machinery, and after seven years, he began standing in for the owner. He married a woman who worked in the post office, and they had two children.

With his senior high school entrance examinations coming up, their younger child said that he wanted to check out a few different schools, so Katō rode the train with him to see a couple of options. The second school they visited lay on the other side of the shopping arcade where Katō had once lived.

Almost all the old shops had vanished from the arcade. Now it was full of chain stores whose main selling point was their affordability. The real estate office had disappeared, and in its place was an apartment building. The school had formerly been an all-boys' school, but had since been rebuilt and turned into a co-ed school, so that it looked entirely different now. All of the teachers that participated in the session for prospective parents and students seemed friendly and kind, and his son seemed to warm to the place.

On the way back, as they walked through the backstreets, Katō told his son that he used to live around here. Huh, the boy replied, apparently uninterested. Even the backstreets were full of new apartment buildings, so Katō assumed that there was no way that his old apartment would still be there, but it was. The temple in front of it was still there also, and the graveyard. Next to it was a parking lot and vacant lot, meaning there was a good view of it from the street.

The apartment hadn't changed from how it had been twenty-five years before. It had been old in the past, and it was still old. And there was a woman sitting at the window who looked a lot like Satō. Wait, that *is* Satō, Katō thought. She had the same clothes and haircut as the last time he'd seen her.

8

**Standing outside a small house, three junior
high students who were skipping school look
toward the nearby train station; ten years pass**

The platform at the station where the express trains
didn't stop was empty.

Only a short section of the platform nearest the station building had a roof, leaving most of its concrete stretch exposed to the elements. With almost no buildings in the vicinity, you could see it from a little way off. The platform was dotted with signs indicating the name of the station, and a few lights on metal poles, but that was it. On hot days, a shimmering heat haze would settle over its surface. Most trains passed straight through—there were only three trains per hour that called at the station, and they were the slow ones, with only two cars. During the daytime, almost nobody got on or off there.

Three junior high students skipping school were standing in a vacant lot in front of a house with a view of the station. They were all looking toward the station. The vacant lot, which stood out front of a house belonging to one boy's grandmother, was separated from the road by a strip of overgrown foliage that shielded it from sight. This was why the three of them had selected it as a place to come from time to time. The grandmother in question didn't reproach her grandson and their friends when they turned up there during school time, but neither did

/ 53

she bring them tea and cookies and such. She simply sat smoking in her favorite chair by the window, looking on at the trains passing through the station as she always did.

"It's all such a pain in the ass," said one of the three as he sat on a cement block in the vacant lot.

"School, you mean?" the grandson asked.

"Mm, no, not exactly."

"I wish the express trains would stop here," the other one who wasn't the grandson said.

At that moment, a blue train was passing through the station without slowing. Perhaps because the wind was blowing in the other direction, it didn't make much sound, despite their proximity. They just felt the ground rumbling slightly.

"Then it'd be easy to get places."

"But you need money," the grandson replied. "If you've got no money then you can't do anything, wherever you go. Wherever you go, it's the same."

"What do you mean, the same?"

"It's no different from being here."

"That's not true. There's loads of shops and stuff, and people, it's not the same as somewhere like here where there's just—nothing."

"What's the point of having shops if you can't buy anything?"

"It's fun to just look, no?"

"If you can't buy any of the stuff, then it's just depressing to look at it. Then you're like, other people can buy this shit, but I can't."

A HUNDRED YEARS AND A DAY / 55

"Is there stuff that you want that much?"

"Not really. Not that I can think of. But I guess there would be, if I could get on an express train."

"So there isn't even anything you want. I don't get what's depressing then."

"You're the one who said there was stuff there." The grandson glared at the station devoid of trains and people.

"There must be stuff there."

The station was quiet, with no sign of anybody around. The sound of the TV carried over from the boy's grandmother's house behind the lot. They heard peals of canned laughter but couldn't make out the words.

"I dunno," one of them said, getting to their feet. "I don't get what you're going on about. The express stops at some stations, and you can go to those if you want to, and if you don't want to, you don't have to. I don't get how you can want something when you don't even know what that thing is."

"You're the one I don't get, going on and on about how you don't get it," the grandson spat out.

"I don't get it, I don't get it, I don't get it," the third one sang in rhythm.

Ten years on, not one of the three lived in the town. The grandmother still lived in the same house, and would sometimes watch the trains passing, which were now less frequent.

Another twelve years on, the station closed. The building was knocked down, the signs and the lights disappeared, and just a platform was left, through which several trains passed over the course of a day. The grand-mother no longer lived in the house, and the grandson moved into her place. He had lived for a while in a big city, but even if he felt envious of the things that other people bought, he never managed to find anything that he really wanted.

Leaning back in the chair his grandmother had always sat in, the grandson looked out at the station that was no longer a station. A new-model silver train slowed down as it slid past, and the grandson, now forty-six, stood up and slid open the glass door. A warm breeze carried in the noise of the train with a slight delay.

9

Family Tree I

My father's grandfather ran an ironmonger's shop in a port town. I never met him. He died fifty years before I was born. They say he got drunk and fell into the sea. My father blamed his own drinking habit on that grandfather of this, but according to my grandmother—my father's mother—the accident happened because my usually abstemious grandfather had, for once, been drinking at a summer festival and lost control. Going by what my grandfather—my father's father—told me on a separate occasion, though, the accident wasn't down to how he couldn't handle his alcohol, but rather to how badly lit that area was after dark. To that day, he couldn't understand why his father would have gone there all by himself.

The ironmonger's shop, which was located right by the port, hasn't been there for a while. When my dad was a kid he lived in the house behind it, but the land where both the shop and the house once stood are now part of the road, which has been expanded. I've never been to the town in question. I have no connection to anyone living there now, so there's no point going, my father always used to say.

I hear there's a hot spring in the town, and on the few occasions I've seen it featured in TV programs, I've thought to myself that I should visit one day, but I've never acted on that impulse. Looking at the town on the TV screen,

I would wonder to myself in which part of the port the ironmonger's was located, but of course there's no way for me to know. My father's mother was born into the family that ran a cafeteria near the port. The cafeteria was there since before the ironmonger's shop. My grandmother's father had started it up with his brother, but when business started thriving and the place got busy, the two brothers had fallen out. The younger one left town and set up another business, which hadn't gone well for him.

The older brother had stayed working in the cafeteria until the day before he died. The place was known for its miso soup made with sea bream scraps, and he'd made that soup on his last day. He made it in just the way that he'd been taught by his mother, back when he was a boy. His mother had moved to the port town from far away to get married. She'd told him there was no sea in the place she'd grown up.

10

**A ramen shop called House of the Future stayed open
for a long time; the other businesses around it vanished,
apartments were built, and people came and went**

The ramen shop stood in the middle of a parking lot.

The building, clad in corrugated metal sheeting, looked flimsy enough to topple over in the wind. It remained standing, though, and even had an upstairs, where the owner lived. The shop's name, Miraiken, or "House of the Future," seemed totally mismatched with its appearance. The owner often joked that it was supposed to be named Rairaiken, a far more standard name for a ramen joint, but that the person creating the sign had made a mistake with one of the characters. None of the regulars knew whether this was true. When asked what "House of the Future" signified, the owner couldn't answer.

When the ramen shop was first built, there were similar businesses on either side of it. They, too, were in what looked like temporary structures; the bar on the right was tilted so that it leaned up against House of the Future. To its left was a dress shop aimed at ladies of a certain age, where the local women would gather to chat. The ramen shop owner had never seen anybody actually make a purchase there.

At the back of House of the Future stood some old wooden row houses. The narrow-fronted buildings, which had different occupants on their first and second floors, had a cramped look about them. The alley on which they stood—so narrow that the row houses seemed to practically touch the houses opposite—was lined with endless doors. Sometimes there would be kids playing in that dingy alley, drawing pictures on the ground in French chalk, but the only more or less permanent fixture was an old man from one of the nearby houses. He carried a stool out into the alley every day. Its vinyl cover was ripped, so you could see the sponge padding beneath. The old man sat on that stool all day. He didn't do anything in particular, just greeted passersby with a "Hello." When it was warm, he would wear just an undershirt, and when it got colder, he'd put on a jacket.

The old man went to House of the Future now and then. His order was always just a bowl of ramen. He barely spoke, but one time he looked at the crime drama playing on the TV and announced that he'd lived there. At that moment, the TV showed a cliff face, where the criminal had been cornered at the show's climax. The old man had apparently been born in a small fishing village close by. "But my dad wasn't a fisherman. He was a drifter, so we didn't stay there for long," the old man mumbled. "Oh really? I visited over ten years ago, but there were all these gift shops and sightseeing boats with their loudspeakers blasting, and it wasn't really how I'd imagined it," the owner said, to which the old man just replied, "Hm."

Two or three years later, people in the neighborhood stopped seeing the old man. Nobody had noticed him move. "When someone or something that should be there isn't there any more, you kind of miss them," a tenant of one of the row houses said as he bolted down his fried rice at House of the Future.

At that time, the row houses contained half the number of residents they once had. There were plans to build apartments in the area, and the estate agent had paid House of the Future's owner numerous visits.

Prices of everything were soaring. This was especially the case for land, which one often heard was going for twice what it had been sold for just two years earlier. Yet House of the Future's customers seemed completely unaffected. Their stories were mostly about feeling stuck—how they were in trouble because their landlord had suddenly announced he was raising their rent, or how they would most likely never be able to afford to buy a house on their salary. When the owner heard from a regular customer that the penthouse apartments in the new building by the station were going for a hundred million yen, the owner took it as a joke. He thought that there was no way someone would buy an apartment for such an exorbitant sum somewhere like here, far from the city center.

He only discovered that it wasn't a joke when the owner of the grocery shop that was opposite the bar sold up and moved out. The grocer had owned a small house by the station, and putting together the money he got from selling that with his eviction compensation money, he raised a handsome sum, with which he bought one of the penthouses.

The area in front of the station was buzzing late into

the night. Drunken men and women strolled around boisterously, and the establishments kept their glitzy Christmas-like decorations up all year round. His customers told him that the entertainment districts in the city center were even rowdier. Hearing their tales of people boasting about their condominiums in foreign cities, and their cars and watches that cost as much as houses, the owner was unable to relate to any of it. That said, he did enjoy hearing the youngsters who bought the cheap ramen and fried rice talking about how they'd just landed a big bit of work, or had got a job working for some director they'd always admired, or had been presented with some award overseas.

Nowadays, more of the customers who came to House of the Future would ask the owner, half seriously, why he didn't sell, what prevented him from cashing in the business and moving into an apartment. But the owner had saved up for a long time, little by little, to afford that place. He had also heard bad things about the real estate agent who'd come by repeatedly. He had no intention whatsoever of selling.

It was around that time that the row house on the corner was set on fire. The flames were extinguished before it could spread, but after being doused in water from the fire truck in midwinter, half of the row houses became uninhabitable. All the locals believed the fire to be the doing of the land sharks, but nobody spoke of the matter publicly. The owner also heard a rumor from several people that the old man who used to sit in the alley hadn't moved away but had gone missing.

A HUNDRED YEARS AND A DAY / *63*

House of the Future started getting silent calls, both during the day and at night. The owner disconnected the phone from the wall. He didn't do deliveries to begin with, so the only complaints he had were from the trades-people he ordered from. Being a lone agent made things easier for him. The guy running the bar next door had a wife and a kid still in elementary school, though, and the woman who owned the dress shop on the other side was the mother of the owner of the shoe shop at the entrance to the shopping arcade. With the man from the bar grow-ing concerned about his wife and child, and the woman from the dress shop being talked round by her son, they sold up their businesses in quick succession.

In no time, both places were demolished. The demo-lition company brought in unnecessarily large machines to tear down those buildings, which were little more than shacks, corrugated metal enshrouding their tired wooden frames. Each time the machines struck the build-ings on either side, House of the Future would tremble, and cracks appeared in its walls. By now, the owner had adopted the attitude that they could do their worst as far as he was concerned. He joked to his customers that if he was killed or the place was burned down, he wanted them to have a big party with the insurance money.

Yet even among the regulars, more and more people were leaving the area to buy apartments or to build their own houses in newly established commuter towns in the suburbs. The people who continued to frequent the place were single middle-aged men, mostly working in build-ing and construction sites close by, and students at the nearby university. There was talk that even the university was going to move.

The area around House of the Future became vacant, and was converted into a parking lot. Similar kinds of parking lots were cropping up in various places across town. Buildings were pulled down here, there, and everywhere, and the residents moved on. Blocks of studio apartments, or those with small bars on every floor from the first to the eighth, went up one after another. All the new buildings were shining white, with marble floors and gold-handled glass doors.

Then the threatening correspondence from the company employed by the real estate agency came to an abrupt halt. With no warning, the owner just stopped hearing from them.

The construction of a nearby apartment building was halted midway. Its half-finished concrete frame, which stretched only as high as the second floor, remained that way for seven years.

With its owner carrying out only the bare minimum when it came to repairs, House of the Future stayed much as it was. Its walls still bore marks left by the roofs of the bar and the dress shop that had once stood on either side of it, and whose structures it had supported. That sign, originally supposed to read "Rairaiken," which instead read "Miraiken," was now peeling pretty badly but remained in place. When it grew dark in the evenings, House of the Future became a solitary glowing presence in the middle of the parking lot.

The area in front of the station gradually grew more

weatherworn. The white buildings that had shot up in such quick succession became dotted with "Rooms Available" signs. You started noticing bags of trash left on the balconies outside the studio flats. The shops in the arcade began closing up, replaced by cheap chain retailers and convenience stores.

House of the Future hadn't changed its prices in decades, and partly because that alone made it something of a rarity, it began attracting more customers. Among them was a young man who would always order ramen, fried rice, and gyoza. The owner assumed he was a student at the nearby university, but after he'd been coming for two years, he confided to the owner that he was a chef, and dreamed of opening up his own place one day. He asked the owner to let him work there. At first the owner refused, but the man seemed unwilling to take no for an answer, and the owner had begun to have problems with his back and kidneys, so in the end he agreed to take the man on part-time.

Almost twenty years passed, and the man who had worked part-time in House of the Future became its owner. The parking lot remained as a parking lot. Across the road stood a tall apartment building, with a conspicuous number of vacant units.

11

A woman hears an announcement on the radio that war has broken out; relatives arrive at her house seeking refuge; when the war ends they leave, then a civil war breaks out

The woman heard the announcement on the radio that war had broken out. Since the beginning of the year, there had been talk that things might come to this, yet the declaration still seemed to arrive out of the blue.

The woman's house was not far from the border, but it lay midway along a mountain road that ran between one town and the next. She was alone when she heard the news, and her surroundings were perfectly tranquil. The sun continued to beam down on the trees that were just coming into bud, and the birds kept up their chirping, just as they had before the announcement. The day was warm and balmy.

Six months later some of the woman's relatives, who had been living in the city, showed up at her door, seeking refuge. The city was subject to the occasional air raid. The area where they lived was still untouched, the wife of the family explained feverishly, but they'd decided to leave when there was bombing in the area around the factory where she worked. The children, perturbed by the sudden change in surroundings, sat silently in a corner of the room. The wife explained that her husband had been sent to a military base near the front line, where he would work not as a soldier but as some kind of communications technician. He was the woman's uncle, but she hadn't seen him since a family funeral over ten years ago.

It was the first time for the woman to meet her uncle's wife, who turned out to be a friendly, talkative person. The woman liked her solitude, and at first found the distance between herself and the wife hard to navigate. But the two women were similar in age, and after a couple of weeks they began conversing casually about the things going on around them, just like school friends.

At the beginning of the war, their country had an overwhelming advantage over the other country, and both the government and the news channels expressed their certainty that the fighting would be over in a matter of months. The people in town, too, echoed this sentiment. Everybody, the woman and the wife included, thought the same, although deep down they likely knew that this was no more than wishful thinking.

After a year had passed, the price of groceries and other everyday items began to increase, and they became harder to come by. The woman grew vegetables on the land around her house, so the situation wasn't desperate, but an acquaintance who had been providing her with milk seemed reluctant to continue. The wife was earning a little money from helping out on a nearby farm. By that point communication from her husband had grown sporadic. The children were still too young for school, but perhaps understanding the significance of the adults' grave and tired demeanor, they occupied themselves quietly in the corners of the house and the garden.

When the wife and children had been living in the woman's house for exactly two years, their city suffered devastating bombing raids. The extent of the damage was even worse than was reported on the radio and in the newspapers, and they heard from people living there that there were virtually no buildings left standing. The base where her husband was working had also been hit, the wife said without altering her expression. The wife had had no contact from her husband since a letter informing her that he'd been moved to a different base on a remote island, but neither had she received an announcement that he'd died or been injured.

One day, the enemy troops came as far as the nearby town. The woman was at home at the time, and the children were also safe at the school they'd just begun attending, but the wife had gone into town to deliver produce from the farm and didn't return. The woman heard the sound of shells echoing, and as night came, planes skimmed low overhead. A faint haze of smoke drifted through the air, and there was a horrible smell. The sky in the direction of the town glowed red.

It was two days later that the wife returned. She'd lost the duffel bag she'd been carrying, and there were bruises and cuts on her face and legs, but she didn't mention what had happened in the town. Nor did she say where she'd been for those two days or what she'd seen.

Yet in the end, that was as far as the enemy invasion progressed. They had extended the front line so far that it had impeded their chains of supply and command,

A HUNDRED YEARS AND A DAY / *69*

said the owner of the farm where the wife had been working. After a while, news arrived that the tide had turned against the enemy.

When the war came to an end a year later, nothing at all remained of the city where the family had been living. The houses, the city hall, the schools, the libraries, the churches—the air raids had left them all in ruins.

It's just the roads that are left, the wife said, after waiting until spring to go and see the state of the place. Only the shapes and the names of the roads are the same as before. Only them.

In the summer, just as the wife had decided to carry on living with her children in the woman's house, her husband came to find her. He had lost a lot of weight, and his face had aged so much that he looked like a different person. He'd sustained a serious injury and been sent to hospital, where he'd caught an infectious disease. For a long time it had been uncertain if he'd pull through. Someone had recommended him for a technician's job in a factory in a port town, he said, where they could now live as a family. For a week after his arrival, the man also lived in the woman's house, eating fruit and vegetables grown locally, and after he'd been restored to life somewhat, the family moved to the port town.

From then on, come the summer, the wife would bring her children and visit the woman's house. Both the wife and the children were delighted that they now had somewhere to spend the summer, and every year the woman looked forward to the season when her relatives would come. The husband's work was going well, the wife said. It seemed as though things had finally settled down for them.

Ten years later, a coup d'état triggered a change in the political system, and the country was plunged into civil war. Anti-government forces began appearing close to the woman's house, and she secured the help of people she knew to move to a country on another continent. In the news she read and saw on TV, it seemed the situation in her home country was only getting worse. She heard from her relatives now living in the port town that they were also thinking of leaving. By that point, the region where the woman had been living was occupied by anti-government forces.

The woman's relatives moved to a different country. They couldn't speak the language there, but it was a small developing nation, and the man had found a good job, said the last letter that the woman received from the wife.

It took almost ten years before the situation in their native country stabilized. Neither the woman nor the wife had any idea what was happening in each other's lives. It was another few years before the woman managed to visit her country. She now had no relatives left there, and stayed only a few days, just to see her place of origin one last time.

Her ship arrived in the port town where her relatives had lived right after the war. The country was now reliant on the financial support of a larger nation, and these days the port town, which had once been old and shabby, boasted an amusement park and tourist facilities.

The woman searched for the street where her relatives had lived, and eventually found what she thought was the right place. It had become an entertainment district for tourists, with most of the old buildings converted into hotels. The woman remembered the wife's words at the time of the first war: *Only the shapes and the names of the roads are the same.* She decided then and there not to go to the valley where she'd lived.

Looking out at the sea from the ship on the way home, the woman thought about the summers when the wife and her children had come to visit—those peaceful, bright summers.

In a country far off across that sea lived the wife and her children. Shortly after arriving there, her husband had died from complications brought on by the disease he'd contracted during the war. Her children were both married, and had three children between them. The wife was soon to give up her job at the garment factory, where she had worked for many years, and move in with her older son's family. During her lunch break, she liked to sit on the bench in the factory garden, which was perched on top of a hill, and look out at the sea. She thought about the country that lay far across that sea, to which she would never return. There were many things she didn't want to remember. But thinking about the days she spent in the woman's house in the valley gave her a feeling of calm. When she thought about those times, she always felt that somewhere far off, the woman was thinking the same thing.

A young married couple now lived in the woman's

house in the valley. The road in front of the house had been converted into a highway, and the couple ran a cafeteria for long-distance truck drivers. They were in the process of deciding what to name their baby, who would soon be born.

12

Ferries that once moored at a certain pier stop running, and for a long time the ferry terminal lies abandoned, but then an affluent investor builds a resort hotel in the area; sometime later a crowd of people watch a new type of aircraft being launched into space from the pier

The ferry pulled into port. There was already a long line of vehicles waiting to board. Usually, most were large trucks, but during the summer vacation, as now, over half were family cars. You could hear the sound of exasperated children crying from some of the cars.

Soaked in the sun's intense rays, the asphalt and the metal vehicles alike exuded a powerful heat. Sweat fell in steady droplets from the chin of the attendant checking tickets. The ferry's hatch opened, and the line of vehicles began to creep forward.

The pier was bustling with activity. The ferry terminal served two different ferry companies, offering a total of seven different routes. The ferries would arrive, load up with crowds of people along with trucks, cars, and cargo, and head out to sea.

A girl whose family was in the habit of visiting her father's hometown over the summer vacation would look forward to the udon and ice cream she'd have on board the ferry. The udon served in cheap pale-blue plastic bowls was a touch overcooked, but eaten at the counter of the udon stall, it always tasted peculiarly good.

The second-class cabin was just a carpeted floor divided into sections, complete with a heap of yellow vinyl pillows that looked like bricks. The father placed a pillow under his elbows, spreading open his newspaper as he directed his gaze at the TV. Once the ferry pulled away from the pier, the reception became so bad that it was hard to make out what was showing onscreen. The mother suffered from seasickness, so she would stroll around to distract herself. The ferry's spacious interior had a games corner with low tables where you could play Space Invaders and mahjong. A chandelier hung in the stairwell leading up to the first-class cabins, which were rarely full. Tagging along with her mother, the girl would persuade her to buy her another ice pop, or ask to take a peek inside the deserted first-class cabins. With its rows of bunk beds, first-class seemed to the girl like a special place, which she longed to enter but never once set foot in. The trip to their father's hometown took six hours on the ferry, and then another two in the car. That village deep in the mountains held a lantern festival for Obon, when the spirits of the dead's return to earth was celebrated.

The last time the girl got on the ferry was in the summer of her third year at university. On a trip she took with the university cycling club, she biked across the prefecture where her father's hometown was.

By that point, there was just one ferry company serving the pier, and only two routes. The construction of multiple bridges, each claiming to be the longest in the world in some way or other, had seen ferry usage plummet, both among transportation companies and regular

A HUNDRED YEARS AND A DAY / *75*

customers. Meanwhile, the cost of fuel was skyrocketing, and several recent newspaper articles speculated that the remaining routes might soon be discontinued.

It was five years since the girl had last disembarked at the port. The house where her grandparents had once lived had been torn down. As one of just a small handful of houses that you had to cross several mountain peaks to get to, its location had been particularly challenging, even within that remote village, and when it became untenable for the child's grandparents to live there by themselves, they moved to a town at the base of the mountain. Not long after moving, though, they both died, one soon after the other.

The entire trip was spent cycling along one mountain road after another, and yet the girl didn't pass through that village where her father had lived until he graduated from junior high school. She didn't even know its exact location. Seeing the view of the mountains from a certain peak, which she crossed on their second day, though, it struck her that it looked identical to the scenery that she remembered. On the way home, her group returned not by ferry but across the bridge that had just opened, and then took the train from the other side.

Three years later, the remaining ferry company suspended operations from the pier.

Once the final bits of business had been wrapped up, part of the terminal building was used as a warehouse for a while and then lay abandoned for about three years. The following summer, the local government joined forces with an event company to hold an arts festival there, which attracted a decent turnout. Right after that, some young people set up a cafe in the building, and a couple of painters started using it as studio space, but neither thing lasted for very long.

Occasionally, boats would pull into the pier to use the port facilities, but mostly it was left untouched. The pier was located a little way down the canal from a larger port that faced the bay, so the luxury cruise ships that were so much in vogue couldn't access it; there was really no use for it any more. Cracks appeared in the concrete, and the mooring poles were left to rust.

Just as the residents themselves were beginning to forget about the abandoned pier, a man passing through while on holiday happened to notice it. He had made an enormous amount of money through his investment company and was now traveling the world. For some reason, he took a liking to the rundown port and came up with the idea of building a holiday resort there. He formed connections with influential people in local government and relevant ministries to secure permission for international yachts to anchor there. The grounds of the resort were encircled by newly planted trees imported from overseas.

An elegant low-rise hotel with spacious rooms was built facing the pier.

On the roof terrace of the restaurant next door, designed by an architect who'd just been awarded an international prize, parties were held almost every night into the early hours of the morning, where DJs played music that carried beyond the grounds.

One summer evening, a couple gazing out at the pier from the roof terrace were picking at a cake with sparklers in it. It was the woman's birthday. A string of large yachts lined the pier. The pier looked very beautiful at night, all lit up in blue. The yacht that the couple had arrived on was the newest model, and it stood out even among all the luxury yachts there. The two were discussing a friend of theirs who was going into space the following summer. The friend would be setting off in a new kind of aircraft that could go into outer space, from a desert in the Middle East that both of them had visited in the past.

Exactly a year later, the pier was filled with people who had assembled to watch shooting stars and the new aircraft going into space. There had been a special dispensation allowing members of the public access to the pier that day, even if they weren't on a yacht or staying in the hotel. A row of stalls set up in front of the hotel sold yakisoba and bright-blue juice. Looking at those stalls modeled on the kind you used to find at summer festivals long ago, children who had never set eyes on the real thing commented to one another how "nostalgic" they found them.

Past midnight, a number of shooting stars cut through the sky, and then they saw the light of the aircraft as it headed into space. The point of yellow light, like that of an especially bright star, slid along its prescribed course and then disappeared into the distance.

Watching that light, the crowd fell silent. Even the young children stayed quiet. It was a very beautiful sight.

Several years later, the investor sold off his business.

The hotel, now part of a major resort chain, was moved to the large port nearby. By that time, it had established itself as a high-end resort, and to avoid marring its image, the building on the pier had been demolished, not a trace of it left behind. The yachts disappeared from the pier as well. The factory on the opposite shore had already disappeared, so none of the yachts had to pass by it any more.

Only the trees flown in from overseas that had encircled the grounds continued to grow, reaching the height of multi-story buildings.

Now that they were finally allowed onto the pier, the local children occasionally went exploring, despite being told at school that the area was dangerous and they mustn't go near it.

A boy in class one of year five at the elementary school was sitting on the pier. He had slipped out of school and was all by himself. It was winter, but the pier got a lot of sunlight and was plenty warm.

Under the dark surface of the water, something was moving. The boy squinted and tried to see what it was but couldn't make it out. He lifted his face and looked toward the mouth of the river. In the distance, out in the bay, he could see a ship. That was the first large passenger ship the boy had ever seen.

13

**All the male children born into a family that ran a
public bathhouse were given a name that included
a specific kanji character, but nobody knew who
first decided that that should be the case**

For generations, the men born into the family that owned
the public bath house at the end of the shopping arcade
leading from the station were given the same kanji character in their name: 正, meaning correct or true. The old
man who now sat in the attendant's booth was named
Shōtarō, written 正太郎; his son was Masahiko, written
正彦; and his grandson, who had just entered elementary
school, was Shōnosuke, written 正之助.

Nobody now knew how far back this tradition of
incorporating the character went, or who had come up
with it. Shōtarō had heard from his father, Shōkichi—
written 正吉—that it was a family rule that the men took
on the character. Hearing this multiple times from an
early age, he had come to believe that the kanji could only
be used for men's names. He didn't go to kindergarten.
Back when he was young, it was rare for children to go
to kindergarten. Seeing Mitchan, who lived in the house
opposite, put on her uniform and head off to the only
kindergarten in the area, he'd felt a sense of envy. With
his world being so small, comprising just the houses in
the immediate vicinity of his own, he'd experienced some
confusion upon entering elementary school. His teacher,

Masaki-sensei—which you wrote 正木—appeared to be a woman, and there was a kid in his class called Masako—written 正子—who looked like a girl. He assumed that these two were really male but were for some reason pretending to be female. He'd heard a story like that. A couple gave birth to a son, but knowing that he'd be killed if word got out that they'd given birth to a boy-child, who could serve as an heir, they'd brought him up as a girl. Eventually the boy who'd been brought up as a girl had grown into a man and avenged his parents, and . . . Shōtarō didn't remember how the story ended, but he remembered vividly how stirred up he'd been by this tale of adventure. For half a year, he'd gone around feeling anxious at the thought that only he knew that Masaki-sensei and Masako Kamimura were really male, and impressing on himself that he better not let the cat out of the bag. When he heard some of the parents talking about how Masaki-sensei had gotten married in the summer vacation, he began to realize that the character wasn't used exclusively for men.

So deeply imprinted in his consciousness was this naming tradition that Shōtarō never thought to ask his father, Shōkichi, who had decided it ought to be that way. He grew up and married a girl from the next town along, to whom his relatives had introduced him. Their first child was a boy, so he'd christened him Masahiko—written 正彦—without even thinking about it. Right before Masahiko was born, Shōkichi died suddenly of a brain hemorrhage, and never got to see his grandchild. Yet he had known that if the child was a boy they planned to

A HUNDRED YEARS AND A DAY / *81*

name him Masahiko, and had seemed pleased by this. Akiko, Shōtarō's wife, thought the name Masahiko had a nice ring to it, and the stroke count was not inauspicious either. Taking a character for a boy's name from that of his father or grandfather was very common, and Akiko was satisfied by Shōtarō's rationale behind the name: the combination of the characters for "correct" and "man" signified that he wanted his son to grow up to be a decent sort of man.

Three years later, when they were expecting their second child, Shōtarō announced that if it was a boy they would name him Masato—written 正人. Akiko objected that having two sons with the character "正" in their names would make things confusing. It was only then that her husband told her that, in his family, all boy's names used that particular character. That was the decision that had been made. You say the decision's been made, but who made it, she asked. Shōtarō replied that it had just always been that way, and they had no choice in the matter. If they started messing around with it now, he'd feel embarrassed to show his face to his father in the afterlife, he said, refusing to budge. My dad's younger brother was named Shoichirō, 正一郎, and his grandfather and all his brothers used the character in their names, but I never heard my mother or my grandmother complaining about it, he added.

To Akiko, who needed to be convinced by the logic of something to get behind it, this convention suddenly seemed like the most unreasonable thing on the planet. There was only a limited number of names containing that particular character; with so many males with those names in a single family, people would get mixed up. And what about the boys—they'll get confused, too! And so the name of their second son remained undecided. The new baby was born with his name still in dispute, and even afterward, Shōtarō and Akiko couldn't agree. The deadline for registering the baby's name approached, and Katsu-toshi, the son of the family who ran the liquor store next door, who had been in Shōtarō's grade at school, stepped in to mediate. It was thus that they decided to bring the "正" character to the end to create the name 康正, which was to be read Kōsei. Masahiko eventually took over the bathhouse; Kōsei got a job in a shipbuilding company and moved far away, and when his son was born four years later, he didn't include the "正" kanji in the boy's name.

At first Masahiko had no intention of taking over the bathhouse, and so he felt that even if he had a son in the future, he wouldn't need to stick to the naming rule. In Masahiko's interpretation, having the character was less proof of genealogical legitimacy, and more a kind of professional nomenclature for those running the bath-house. He'd read in a book about artisans of certain tradi-tional crafts whose names were passed down through the generations, so that they'd be referred to as "Blah-blah-blah XII," and so forth. When a new person assumed the post, they'd alter their name in the family register. Masa-hiko was impressed by this, but at the same time couldn't imagine how it would feel to go as far as officially chang-ing your name in the interests of preserving tradition. He thought about it for three days. The conclusion that he came to, in a flash, was that if he wasn't going to take over the bathhouse then he didn't need to carry on the character-giving tradition either.

He didn't discuss the matter with his father, Shōtarō. He could easily imagine his short-tempered father flying off the handle if he did. He struggled, also, to tell his father of his ambition to become a pilot. As he kept this desire to himself, he mulled over the fact that neither his grades nor his eyesight were good enough to make it happen, and gave up on the idea. After leaving high school, he worked for five years or so in a wholesale food company, married a girl called Mitsuko who worked in the admin department, and then returned home to take over the bathhouse. Shōtarō was delighted. That night he stayed up late drinking, saying, you are my son after all. You inherited the kanji in your name, and you inherited the bathhouse.

Masahiko's first-born child was a girl. He realized that he was relieved by this, because it meant he didn't have to decide whether or not to include the character in her name. They named her Yōko—written 陽子—whose characters mean "sun" and "child." Their second child, born two years later, was a boy. After deliberating endlessly, Shōtarō decided to call him Shōnosuke: 正之助. The name, which had a slightly old-fashioned ring to it, was the name of the main character in a manga Shōtarō had loved as a child. Hearing about the family's naming tradition, Mitsuko seemed delighted by it, saying that it was important to treasure old customs, and it was wonderful to inherit a tradition like that. Observing her reaction, Shōtarō felt relieved that his son had married a good egg. He rebuilt the house at the back of the bathhouse so that it could accommodate two generations of the family, living separately.

Shōnosuke entered elementary school. He was the smallest in his class. He was short-sighted and wore glasses, and the other kids called him a dweeb. When asked to write a composition for homework entitled "My Dream for the Future," Shōnosuke wrote that his dream was to become an actor. He liked watching the reruns of period dramas that were on TV when he came home from school. Mitsuko told him that acting wasn't a career for a man to seriously consider. It was fine to dream of that for now, she said, but by the time you leave elementary school you need to start thinking more practically about your future. The location here is so good, you could renovate the bathhouse and create one of those with entertainment facilities that are so popular these days, your dad has a good head for commerce, and you could develop it together, she went on. It'd be best if you took over the family business, you've got the character in your name after all. Mitsuko went about the physically demanding job of running the bathhouse without complaint. She would clean it every day, work that went into the early hours of the morning, and would then get up the earliest of all the family to make everyone breakfast.

By the time Shōnosuke graduated from high school, the number of bathhouse customers had dropped off considerably. Shōtarō had back problems, and could no

A HUNDRED YEARS AND A DAY / *85*

longer sit in the attendant's booth. He spent more time stretched out in the living room, in the house behind the bathhouse. Shōnosuke continued to dream of becoming an actor, but no longer spoke of his dreams to his family. Almost daily, he would go to the cinema in the shopping arcade, and then rent old movies from the video shop on his way home. Mitsuko had stopped talking to him about taking over the bathhouse. Still, her desire for him to enter the business world remained strong. His grades were good, and his teachers didn't doubt that he would go on to study at the local national university. Masahiko somehow sensed that his son was bound for some far-flung place. Yet he never said to him that there was no need for him to take over the bathhouse. Just as when deciding whether to include the character in the boy's name, he found it hard to take action that entailed altering or ending things. The bathhouse had been the place Masahiko had played as a child and worked for most of his adult life, and he harbored a deep affection for it. He also felt sad about no longer seeing the old men who had come every day, one after another, when he was young.

Shōnosuke entered the local national university but dropped out in his second year, then left home to join a small up-and-coming theater company. Mitsuko wept and opposed his decision, but Masahiko said nothing, simply seeing him off in silence. For a while, Shōnosuke lived in obscurity, working at a liquor store and living in an apartment without a bath, which was something of a rarity by that point. To bathe, he went to the local public bathhouse. He would always go around midnight. For some reason the people who came at that hour all had tattoos on their backs. At home, he'd never been inside the big baths. The bathhouse, for his family, had been a place of work. Bathing at his leisure as a customer, he came to think that the institution of the bathhouse was a very good thing. It was a strangely comfortable place, where strangers soaked together in the hot water, then silently returned to their respective homes.

Into his thirties, Shōnosuke got good reviews for a supporting role in a TV series, and he was finally able to just about get by on his acting alone. People often remarked that they'd been sure Shōnosuke was a stage name. He would reply by explaining that in his family, the "正" character was passed down through generations, but that he didn't know why or when the tradition had started.

Around the time that Shōnosuke moved into an apartment with a glass-walled bathroom, Shōtarō died. He had been in a nursing home for a long time. Shōnosuke's grandmother, Akiko, looked forward to watching Shōnosuke on TV, but of late she had forgotten that he was her grandson and seemed to think he was an actor she'd been fond of when she was young. On the night of Shōtarō's wake, Masahiko told Shōnosuke that he was going to close the bathhouse. The recent spike in fuel costs had been the last straw. Shōnosuke told Masahiko about his spell frequenting the local bathhouse when he'd lived in an apartment without a bath. Hearing this, Masahiko realized that he would have liked to have had the experience of visiting a bathhouse, too.

They initially planned to demolish the building, which was close to eighty years old, but their daughter, Yōko, won out against the others' opposition and renovated the building to create a cafe and event venue. She added on a guesthouse, and overseas tourists began coming to stay. The tiled bathrooms were repurposed; the women's bath was used as a stage, and the men's as the counter for a bar. Yōko would tell people with a smile how lucky she was to be born into a family that had run a bathhouse.

At the age of forty-two, Shōnosuke married the film director Terumi Imai, and the couple had a son the following year. Terumi gave the boy a name that she said had come to her in a dream. It didn't contain the "正" character.

14

Daughter Tales II

Where I'm working at the moment, the daughter began in a very ordinary tone of voice, they always have the radio on, even when everyone's working. It's always set to the same AM station where people call in for life advice and stuff. Don't you think it's weird to have that on when people are working? Ah, really? the mother said. In the company I worked in when I was young they kept the radio on too, but it was tuned to a music station. Really? In the office? Don't you think it's weird for there to be any sound other than that of people working? I think it's really strange. Is it really that strange? the mother said, searching her memory. She had worked in two places, and they'd kept the radio on in both. In both, they'd set the radio to an FM station playing upbeat music, so in that sense the situation was different, but she felt that a totally silent office would be harder to work in. Yet her daughter seemed so convinced that the workplace should be a place of tranquility that she kept quiet and listened to what she had to say.

Back when the mother spent all day at work listening to hit songs, not at all the sort of music she was into, she never spoke with her own mother about her workplace, or her job. She knew that if she did, her mother would be quick to encourage her to quit. In fact, regardless of whether she spoke about it or not, her mother would

A HUNDRED YEARS AND A DAY / *89*

tell her on what felt like a daily basis to give up her job. This was because she had turned down the admin role at a securities bank that her mother had found for her through relatives, and instead taken up a position at the graphic design firm where she wanted to work—and, to make things worse, accepted a position as a non-permanent member of staff. Her mother would often remark that the men working at a glitzy workplace like that were good for nothing, and if she kept working there she'd miss out on her chance to marry. Recalling her own youth, her mother would tell her that she should be in a workplace with serious people, like she herself had done.

The staff at the union office where her mother worked for just two years when she was younger had played volleyball together during the summer vacation, and someone had occasionally put the radio on then. Everyone knew the hit songs that were playing, and sometimes they sang along. When she went home, she told her mother excitedly what had happened. Her mother had said, you young people today are so lucky. In the factory where I worked, there was only the sound of the machines, and if you were found talking at all, you'd get into such trouble.

15

Two friends were in the habit of visiting a certain repertory cinema every month; before the screening, they always went to eat ramen, gyoza, and fried rice at a ramen place nearby; once there was someone in one of the movies that they watched who was the spitting image of one of the two friends

Before going to the cinema, the two would always stop in at the local ramen place.

The cinema in question was a repertory cinema, which screened movies three months or half a year after they came out. Once a month, they had a late show where they screened classic films, or the work of a European director, or something along those lines.

It was these late screenings that the pair attended. The show usually started at 9 pm. The friends would meet an hour and a half earlier in the bookshop in the underground passage that joined up with the station. They would go to eat ramen, gyoza, and fried rice in the ramen restaurant by the street exit of the underground passage, and then head to the cinema.

The restaurant served tonkotsu ramen—ramen made with pork-bone broth—and its sign featured an illustration of a smiling pig. It had been there from the time that the friends, who had met at university, had started going to the cinema, but it didn't seem to be all that old. In the evening when they visited, there were lots of solo diners on their way home from work. The solo diners mostly drank beer, but the two friends were united in the opinion that beer didn't go well with ramen.

The cinema was on the top floor of an old brick building. The elevator was painfully slow. When one of them pushed the thoroughly scratched button imprinted with the number seven, the elevator would take so long that they began to fear they'd never get there. When the door opened and they stepped out, there was no sales counter and no projection room in sight. Sitting at a flimsy folding table that served as a reception desk was a plain-looking woman whose face they found it impossible to memorize however many times they saw her. She would tear them off perforated paper tickets and hand them over. Behind her sat two projectors, with nothing to protect them, and large film cans in piles on the floor.

In the screening room, blackout curtains were drawn across the walls, and metal chairs were set out in rows. It always made one of the friends think of a school gym. When the movie was over, the two would head back to the station via the underground passage, and take different train lines home. They repeated this routine every two or three months for five years.

Once, a movie that they watched at the cinema featured an actor who looked exactly like one of the two friends.

It was a Taiwanese movie. In the scene in question a boy, who was the film's protagonist, went to the cinema with a classmate he'd just started dating. The light from the projectors spread through the dark of the cinema.

Motes of dust danced in its whiteness. The light picked out the slightly nervous face of the boy, and the face of the girl sitting next to him, engrossed in what was happening onscreen and apparently oblivious to the boy's presence. It wasn't clear what film they were watching, but it appeared to be some kind of romantic comedy in English.

The person who looked exactly like one of the friends was sitting in the row behind the couple, diagonally behind the girl. It was dark and the girl's face wasn't fully in focus, so you would have thought that it would have been difficult to make out her features, but when one of the friends caught sight of her she almost gasped. She'd heard it said that there were three people in the world that looked exactly like any individual. If that was the case, she thought, then this had to be one of her three. It even occurred to her that perhaps she'd been to that cinema and been filmed without her permission, ending up in the movie without knowing it. She nudged her friend and whispered, look! She looks like me.

Not understanding what she was saying, the friend was confused at first, but after scanning the screen and catching sight of the face, he too almost gasped. You're right, he whispered, and was on the verge of asking, when did you go to Taiwan? The scene in the cinema lasted only two or three minutes. The boy reached for the girl's hand in the dark of the cinema, but her expression didn't shift in the slightest. She carried on staring fixedly at the screen. The shot showed the couple straight on, so the two friends felt as though they themselves were being watched by the young boy and girl—not to mention by the doppelgänger behind the couple.

That proved to be the last trip the friends made to the cinema together. Neither of them suspected at the time that it would be, but then two weeks later, there was an announcement at one of the friends' workplaces that they would be transferring offices to another city. The friend in question hurriedly made preparations, and moved away.

The other friend went to the cinema alone three more times after that. She didn't go for ramen before the show, but instead had a coffee in a nearby cafe.

It was a cold day, near the end of winter. When the movie ended and the friend stepped into the elevator hall, the door to the fire exit that was usually shut stood open. As she approached it, she caught a glimpse of the night sky.

The landing outside the fire exit looked as if it were floating there in the darkness. The building behind it, which had been there when she'd visited last month, had since been demolished, and in its place was a large plot of vacant land. The walls of the surrounding buildings that faced onto the plot looked very different from their street-facing walls, having only air vents and tiny windows on staircases. Though it was in the city center, you didn't sense the presence of any people.

It was like a deep lake of diluted darkness had opened up in that one spot. The cold wind rushed past, leaving the friend unsteady on her feet. The feeling frightened her, but she remained there, gazing out into the darkness. The light of the windows from distant skyscrapers twinkled.

The old brick building with the cinema inside was

demolished half a year later. The recession brought the redevelopment plans to a standstill, however, and it remained as a vacant lot for a while.

It was ten years before the new building was finally completed.

At that time, the friend who had remained in the city was in Taipei for a three-night holiday. She visited restaurants and shops with her friends, stopping into a huge bookstore that was open until late at night.

While having her future read by a fortune teller on the street, she suddenly remembered how she'd seen someone identical in a scene from a movie. That movie had been set in Taipei. The city as it was now seemed a world away from how it had appeared in that film. Whereabouts had that cinema been? It must be somewhere here, she thought with strange conviction. If the film had been shot not long before it had been screened, then her doppelgänger would be about the same age as she was.

The friend had gone on to see many more movies after that one and been abroad several times, but had never met anyone that looked identical to her, nor had anyone else reported encountering such a person.

The following day, she visited a converted building that had originally been constructed by the Japanese government during the war. The building now housed a gallery, cafes, and shops selling trinkets, and it was swarming with young people and tourists. She was leaving that evening, so she looked for souvenirs to give people when she returned home.

In one corner of the building stood a display of materials dating back to when the place was built, and a timeline showing the history of the building. Approaching it, a photo caught her eye. Employees of the distillery that this building had once housed stood in rows, as in a school photograph. The photograph was black and white, and had been blown up on the panel so that it was quite blurry. The child standing to the far left looked like the person in that film. Squinting at the picture, she recalled the dark, vacant plot of land she'd seen on the last day she'd been to the cinema.

The other friend was back in the city he'd once lived in on business. He was only staying two nights, and his schedule was packed with work appointments, so he hadn't even thought of getting in touch with the friend he'd once been close to, or of visiting any of the places he'd frequented when he was young.

On the way to the station from his business hotel, he passed the spot where the cinema used to be. He didn't realize it at first. It was only when he was waiting at the crossing for the lights to change that it occurred to him that he recognized his surroundings, and turned around.

A tall building stood where the cinema had once been. Reflecting the sky, its glass front shone a bright blue.

The two friends had grown apart and were no longer in touch. Sometimes they'd recall a particular movie that they'd seen together in that cinema. At those times, they'd want to talk with someone about what they'd seen, but would have the feeling that nobody would get what they were trying to say, apart from the person they'd been to the cinema with, so they didn't say anything.

16

A river whose bank was visible from the second-floor window of a house floods during a typhoon and almost bursts its banks; when the house was first built, there was nothing around it but fields; even further back in the past, there were no people living there

You couldn't see the river itself from the second-floor window.

Kyōko was in the habit of gazing at the riverbank every morning from her east-facing bedroom. People passed by, walking their dogs: a man, a woman, a child; a Shiba Inu, a mongrel, a Pomeranian. A group of students went jogging past, wearing the regulation tracksuits for the nearby senior high school. A gray heron stood perfectly still. Crows came and went. All of this was repeated, day in and day out.

To get to her elementary school, to get to her junior high school, and then, eventually, to get to the station from which she caught a train that took her to her senior high school, Kyōko had to walk up onto the bank of the river and cross the bridge. She couldn't count how many times she'd come and gone across the river, first on foot when going to elementary school, and then on her bike to get to junior high and, subsequently, the station. When she climbed up onto the bank, the river came into view. There wasn't usually much water there; the reed-strewn riverbed was wider than the river itself. Sometimes there were ducks and herons. On sunny days, the sunlight would reach the bottom of the shallow riverbed, where the shadows cast by the rippling water created patterns. Sometimes she stood there, watching it.

At night the river was cast into darkness, making it impossible to gauge its depth. Kyōko could hear the sound it made. She wondered why it was that you could hear it more clearly at night than in daylight, but she never asked anyone.

In September of Kyōko's third year in senior high school, a weather front connected with a typhoon brought rainfall heavier than Kyōko had ever experienced before to the area, and the water level rose in what seemed like no time. An evacuation order was issued, and Kyōko took shelter in the community center, along with her parents and younger sister. She saw a couple of her classmates in the main hall. People spread out the blankets they'd been given across the floor, but they didn't sleep, just sat there for hours. There was a terrifying noise coming from outside. The howling of the wind, loud enough to interrupt their conversations, continued into the early hours of the morning. The news program playing on a TV in a corner of the hall showed images of the river. The reporter was standing a good distance downstream from Kyōko's house, where the river was wider, and there the water level had risen enough to flood the grassy fields on both sides.

Will we be okay around here, do you think, the residents who'd taken shelter in the village hall whispered to one another. Someone's gone to take a look, somebody said. A couple of people were angered by this, saying, going to the river at a time like this, what are they think-ing? What if they get swept away?

Watching the TV reporter shouting his commentary at a volume that felt performative, Kyōko thought of the riverbank. She pictured the moment when the dark water rose above the bank that she looked out at every day. She imagined the banks on both sides of the river being breached, the surging water rushing into the towns and fields, stripping away the soil and toppling houses, as she'd seen at some point on the news. The scene played on a loop in her mind.

Her sister, Asumi, was engrossed in the handheld game console she'd brought with her. I can't believe that the sound of the rain and the news that the banks might be breached doesn't affect you at all, Kyōko said to Asumi, but Asumi just grunted in reply. When she got bored with the console, she fell asleep.

In the end, it was a narrow miss, and there was no flooding. Early the next morning, Kyōko and family returned home under a blue sky, which signaled that the typhoon had passed. Kyōko went up to her second-floor room and looked at the riverbank from the window. There were a number of people standing there who'd come to inspect the state of the river. The water still wasn't visible from the window. For a while, Kyōko found it impossible to accept that the sight of the riverbank crumbling and the powerful tide rushing in, which she'd imagined so many times with as much clarity as if it were real, was not what was actually there. They'd received the news that, even on a day like today, school would open as normal, and so Kyōko began getting ready. Saying that it was dangerous to pass by the river, her father gave her a lift to the station in the car, taking a roundabout route. What Kyōko had really wanted was to go over the bridge as usual, she thought as she looked up at the clear sky.

Back when Kyōko's father had bought the house, the surrounding area had been mostly fields. There had been improvement work done on the river just a few years earlier, and a promenade had just been created along one side. His relatives and acquaintances advised that it was dangerous to live so close to the river, but he decided to trust what the developer said, namely that it was okay because the house was built on a mound, and there was a dam upstream that controlled water levels and would prevent the flooding that had taken place in the past.

Before moving into the brand-new two-story house, Kyōko's father visited it on his own. He had married the year before, and he and his wife were expecting a child in six months' time. He had taken out a loan and bought a house—it seemed fair to say that everything in life was going very smoothly. He didn't worry about whether it was okay for everything to be going this smoothly. His colleagues were in similar positions, and he felt like that was just an average sort of life, like everybody had.

The unfurnished house was spacious. After walking around thinking about where he'd put the dining table, the TV, and so on, he went out onto the second-floor balcony. He could see the riverbank from there. The grass was still only sparse, and the bare concrete blocks shone white.

A bicycle went racing past. After a little while, a dog walked by. It was a big white mongrel. Squinting, he made out a red collar. He looked around, but he couldn't see anybody that appeared to be its owner. The dog was walking in a straight line from right to left, stepping lightly. It moved over to the bridge, without looking around, as though that were its daily routine. It seemed to him as if the dog crossed the bridge.

I'll have to be careful when I take my children to the riverbank, it might be best to get in touch with the local authorities, he thought as he smoked a cigarette on the balcony, then went into the room and lay down on the floor. It smelt of brand-new tatami.

A hundred years previously, the riverbank was lower. Every three or four years the river would flood, immersing the shoots growing in the paddy fields. People complained to the village office, but for a long time, no improvements were made.

Even further back in time, the area was all untended fields and woodland. There was no riverbank. The river itself was meandering, and you could often see fish.

Occasionally, the men who lived in the nearby village would come to the river to fish, but most of the time there was no sign of anybody around. One day, a young man from another village grew unsure of how to get home. He lost sight of the path that led through the field of tall reeds, and then the sun began to set.

Left with no other choice, he decided to sleep under a large tree near the river. Luckily the season was warm, so he lay down on the ground, taking the roots sticking out of the ground as a pillow. The night sky was filled with stars. He heard the sound of some kind of wild beasts calling, which spooked him, but he was exhausted from all the walking and didn't feel like moving.

As he was dozing off, he heard the sound of flowing water. The river had been so gentle—why could he hear it so loudly now? It hadn't rained for a while, and the water level had been very low when he'd seen it earlier. The sound of the water echoed loudly around him, and he heard the rustling sound of the wind passing through the reeds.

When the man woke up the following morning, he found that he was lying on the riverbank, despite thinking himself to be under a tree. Sitting up, he saw there were several fish laid out next to him. This freaked him out, and he hurriedly moved off. When he parted the reeds he instantly found the narrow path, as if all his troubles from the previous day had been a dream. Returning to his village, the man told everyone he met that he'd been kidnapped by a kappa, a green river-dwelling spirit.

Even further back in the past, there were no people living there, nor any large animals. When the wind blew from the south, it would always rain.

17

In a second-hand store unimaginatively called "Second Hand," Abbie finds a book of manga and a novel from Japan; when she shows them to a classmate who can read Japanese, he tells her that the note written on the novel's last page is a love letter

In the shopping mall on the outskirts of town was a store selling second-hand items.

The shopping mall was a small-scale affair, mostly discount stores and fast-food outlets. Only the parking lot was disproportionally large. In one corner of the lot stood the second-hand store. It was a habit of Abbie's to pop in every couple of weeks on her way home from the university.

Abbie had first visited the store before the semester began. On her third day after moving to this rural town, a girl named Karen, who lived in the apartment just beyond hers in the student housing, had driven her there. Karen had a clear idea of what she wanted: she was looking for an old wooden stool to arrange her things on and had found the second-hand store while searching online. In the end, though, even after making her way several times around the capacious shop floor, she could find neither what she was imagining, nor something different from what she'd been imagining but that she just fell for at first sight. That phrase—"different from what I'd imagined but that I just fell for at first sight"—was one that

Karen used about her boyfriend as the two girls wandered around, looking through the collections of cheap storage boxes and mismatched shoes that people had left behind. Karen was very talkative, and Abbie mostly just listened and made appropriate responses. Abbie had been thinking that she'd buy some dishes if she found any plain ones, but the only dishes in the store were either emblazoned with cartoon characters or gold-rimmed with lavish floral patterns. In the end, Karen bought a backpack made by an outdoor brand, and Abbie a pair of tumblers still in their gift box, and that was it.

Karen never returned to the store, but Abbie took to visiting occasionally in the blue second-hand car she'd bought, partly as an excuse to practice her driving, which she didn't feel very confident about. From time to time, she would stumble on real finds in the second-hand store: the blue rack whose paint was chipped to just the right degree still stood in the kitchen, and the red high heels that fit her perfectly had been ideal for a Christmas party. Most of the items, though, were pretty low quality. The store was overflowing with clothes and kitchenware that wasn't old enough to seem stylishly retro, and instead just looked slightly dated—items that were new enough but didn't instill any desire in her to take them home and use them.

Not infrequently, Abbie would look at an item and wonder what the original buyer had liked about it. Even if it was purchased as a stopgap, there must have been something about it to recommend it to someone. There was no shortage of objects in the world, and if you went to one of those huge discount stores such as you found in the mall, there were many different kinds of shirts and plates, so the people who bought these items must at least have chosen them from a range of alternatives.

Standing there in the second-hand store, Abbie would sometimes find herself imagining the moment those particular objects had first been selected from the myriad items lining the shelves, all slightly different from one another. She could never see the buyers in their entirety, but on several occasions she felt she could picture their hands, reaching out toward the items.

Whether or not those hands were the reason that Abbie kept returning every couple of weeks to the store, Abbie herself wasn't sure. At some point, an Asian food store had opened up in the mall, and she liked perusing the ingredients there. She often bought things she needed in the discount store, and there was really nowhere else to go unless you drove all the way to the next town, so maybe it was really no more than an entertaining detour.

One time Abbie stumbled upon a book of Japanese manga on the shelves in a corner of the store. It wasn't translated into English. Flipping through the pages, she was able to glean that it was a kind of love story between a girl and a boy. On the shelf beside the manga was another Japanese book. This one looked like a novel, its pages covered in dense script. On the cover was a photograph of an old Japanese house, photoshopped to look like an illustration. Abbie couldn't read a word of either book, but they each cost less than a chocolate bar, so she bought them and took them home.

Back in her dorm room, Abbie opened the books to find they were as incomprehensible as ever. The manga seemed to end at a point midway through the action, so she presumed it had a sequel. It didn't say "1" or "2" or anything that might have indicated that on the cover, she thought to herself, dissatisfied. With the novel, it was hard to guess even what type of story it was. Abbie had read a book by a Japanese author in translation, and had liked the way that reality seemed to blur with the world of dreams, but she didn't understand the Japanese language at all. It was made up of different kinds of scripts, and there weren't even any spaces to indicate where one word ended and another began.

The new semester started and in one of her classes Abbie met a boy who liked manga and who could read a decent amount of Japanese, so she showed him the manga and the novel she'd bought in the second-hand store. A frown formed on boy's long, pallid face as he flipped through the pages, and after looking something up on his laptop, he informed her that it was a very popular manga from the eighties, which had been made into a film. He added, unnecessarily as far as Abbie was concerned, that it was a traditional love story, and that the heroine's boyfriend dies at the end. The novel, he said, was the story of someone who took a trip tracing their parents' roots, a mother and father from whom they had been separated at birth.

The handwritten note penciled into one of the pages of the novel was a love letter, the boy informed her curtly. He added impassively that the book's owner was writing of their feelings for a lover living far away, and there was no way of telling if it ever reached them.

Abbie looked at that book quite a lot but could never read it. Now and then she thought about learning Japanese, but she was always busy with her studies or her part-time job and never got around to it.

As graduation approached, Abbie found a job in the city near where she'd grown up. Soon she would have to move out of the apartment where she'd lived for four years. Abbie took most of the items in her room to the second-hand store. It was her first time to sell anything there. She had anticipated she wouldn't get much for her stuff, but the price they offered her was so low that she imagined it barely covered the cost of the gas to drive there. She deliberated a little, but decided to sell the Japanese manga and novel that had sat on her bookshelf the whole time. She imagined someone else might find them.

It took three years for another hand to reach out and claim the books. This one belonged to the daughter of a Japanese academic who'd found a job at the university. Generously enough, the parents of a girl in the same class at middle school who lived in the next town gave the girl a tour of various local places, one of which was the second-hand store. Seeing that familiar script on the bookshelf in the corner, the girl immediately reached for the two books. The manga and the novel had sat in the exact same place for the three years since Abbie had parted with them.

The girl used her allowance to buy the books, which were in pretty good condition considering their age.

English still felt unfamiliar to her, and in this small town with hardly any Japanese people, the books were somehow reassuring.

The narrative of the manga was hackneyed, and the volume ended midway through the story, but she didn't dislike the illustrations. She started reading the novel, but it was a sentimental kind of book, full of old people feeling nothing but regrets, so she abandoned it quickly without having read even a third.

One day, while cleaning the girl's room, her mother picked up the novel and opened it. She didn't read many novels, but the story was set in the part of Japan her own mother had come from, and taken by a kind of nostalgia, she began to read it right away. In a note scribbled in pencil on a blank page, someone expressed their regret about not having visited a certain relative before they died. The girl's mother could imagine how the contents of the novel would have induced those kinds of feelings in the reader, but it wasn't clear from the note what kind of person had written it, or to whom it was addressed. *I wish I could have seen you again*, the note said twice.

The father's contract at the university came to an end, and the mother went along with the daughter to the second-hand store. The manga they put in their luggage to take home, but the novel was sold on again, along with their furniture and other bits and bobs.

The store remained open after their return to Japan. The fast-food outlets in the mall were replaced by other fast-food outlets, and an Indian supermarket opened up next to the Asian one, but the second-hand store continued buying and selling those unremarkable, insignificant items just as before. Even after the company that owned the big discount stores folded and the shopping mall itself closed down, the second-hand store in the corner of the parking lot by the road remained. It had already seen several different owners, and none of the customers remembered the original one. As long as people moved to the town and left again, they had things to buy and things to sell—it was as simple as that.

18

After two years in a first-floor apartment, the tenant realizes that a certain cat would pass along the street in front at precisely the same time each day; following the cat, the tenant sees it disappear into a vacant house; when the tenant first moved into the apartment, the house wasn't vacant

In the evening the cat would make its way across the narrow street in front of the apartment building. It was a tabby, neither skinny nor fat, with no distinguishing features to speak of, and when the tenant in the first-floor apartment saw it, she paid it no particular notice. It was only after living there for two years that the tenant realized the cat passed by at almost exactly the same time each day. She couldn't quite remember when she'd begun to notice the cat, but she definitely remembered seeing it in the summer, and back in the spring.

The cat always came walking from the corner where the parking lot was, and would vanish beneath the gates of a vacant house at the end of the street. Several times, the tenant attempted to follow the cat but, once it entered the grounds of the vacant house, she didn't know where it went next. Perhaps the cat was using it as a place to sleep, she thought, but she had never seen any indication that someone in the neighborhood was feeding it.

When the tenant commented to a friend that she hadn't been aware that cats were creatures of such set habits, the friend seemed astonished. The friend's family had kept cats since before she was born—not just one, either, but two or three at a time. The friend now lived alone, but she'd brought one of the cats from home to her new place. It was a black cat, terribly shy. When the tenant visited her friend, the cat would always hide in the closet, so she'd seen it only once.

Well, how could I know that about cats if I've never had one, the tenant asked sulkily. Besides, she argued, people who have cats say that they like the fact they're so easygoing, don't they? The friend replied that this clearly came from someone who was not a cat person. People who don't understand cats will declare knowingly that cats don't take to people, or that they're more attached to places than to people, or that they don't show affection like dogs do, she said, but when I was growing up my cats would always be waiting in the entrance for me when I got home, and the one I'm living with now wasn't fazed at all by the move from my parents' house, because I was there with him.

Yet hearing about cats from the friend didn't help the tenant to understand where the tabby appeared from and where it went. When fall came, and the sun began setting earlier in the day, the hour of the cat's passage also grew earlier. The tenant felt strangely impressed to discover that the cat was moving in accordance not with time as it appeared on the clock, but with more natural rhythms. The tenant, who worked at home as a writer, began taking a walk at the same time that the tabby passed by.

Shortly after the tenant emerged from her apartment

one evening, the cat turned the corner into the parking lot. Its gait seemed slightly hurried. It walked with its eyes pinned straight ahead, not turning its head to look around. Noticing the tenant, it stopped, and slowly turned its head toward her. The tenant returned its gaze. So long as the pair's eyes remained locked, the tabby didn't move. Its front leg, which it had begun to extend, was frozen in position. She had learned from watching the cat that in dim light a cat's pupils expand to black orbs. She had previously believed that their pupils were always vertical slits. Feeling bad for staring so intently, the tenant looked away and the cat continued walking, as if it had just been on pause and now someone had hit the play button. It passed under the gate of the vacant house and disappeared from sight.

When the tenant had first moved in, there were signs that someone was living in the now-vacant house. Several times she had seen the gates slightly ajar, with a bike parked in front. She didn't recall ever seeing lights on in the windows, though, and there was no sign of life apart from the bicycle. Of course she'd never seen the people who lived there.

It was a two-story house with no decorative features—neither a traditional wood construction steeped in a sense of history, nor a modern concrete cube declaring its designer credentials. The textured-plaster walls and sliding windows were the kind that you could see in any neighborhood. As the tenant watched the cat disappear, it occurred to her how difficult it must be to crawl beneath the floorboards of this house to sleep. Maybe the vacant house was just a stage on its journey, and the cat had a destination beyond. Its fur looked glossy enough, so it must be getting fed somewhere. The tenant's observation of the tabby continued, but just before winter came, she had to return suddenly to her family home. Her father had taken ill, and they needed her help with the family business. On the day before she moved out, the tenant watched the cat disappear into the vacant house.

The house had definitely not been fully vacant when the tenant moved into her apartment. Its owner had been in and out of hospital for six months, and her second daughter, who lived close by, would come round to collect the mail and clean the house. When the tenant moved in, the owner was midway through a final, protracted stay in hospital. For a while after the owner died, the daughter would come by to sort out the house. During that time, the daughter would also spot the cat from time to time. While cleaning the house, she would open the glass door to the garden—though really that space barely deserved the appellation, described more accurately as a long thin gap between house and wall—and the cat would stroll past. It always approached from the direction of the gate, using the stack of empty flower pots as a platform from which to jump up onto the concrete wall, and walked off toward the house at the back. The daughter was always amazed by the cat's light-footed movements when it leapt onto that five-foot wall.

The daughter had never had a cat, either. When she was a child, growing up in this house, there'd been a dog. Her older brother had rescued it, on his way home one day from junior high school. He said that it had followed him home from near the school. They named the dog Goro. At first it was small and round, but it was a mongrel and grew to be larger than expected, and walking it became a lot of work. It was mostly their father who walked the dog. The daughter, who had just started elementary school when Goro arrived, loved him very much but had always wanted a cat. Both her parents, however, hated cats, and later, so did her husband, and so her wish had never been fulfilled. Whenever she noticed the tabby, she would be taken by the desire to see it up close, but if she tried approaching, it would run away.

The tabby, having leapt up onto the wall, now made its way along the top. Another cat lived in the house behind. It was a pure-white long-haired cat. The people in that house were careful not to let it outside, and it was always sitting in a window on the second floor. When the tabby looked up, the white cat would look down.

The window in which the white cat was sitting was in the bedroom belonging to the daughter of the house. An only child, she had left home to attend university in a different city and subsequently found a job there, but her room in the family home remained as it was. During the long holidays, the daughter would return home for three or four days. She would lie around in her room, petting the cat. The cat had been given to them by someone her mother knew, back when the daughter was in junior high school. When the kitten first arrived, she was hesitant to touch it, concerned that a creature that small might die if she so much as laid a finger on it. The white kitten grew rapidly, and was soon bigger than her friend's cat. The daughter found the cat's presence reassuring. Now almost fifteen, the cat no longer rushed over to play with its favorite toys when the daughter offered them, but merely glanced in their direction. Her mother had told her that when she wasn't there, the cat would spend practically the whole day sitting by the window. The daughter wanted to bring the cat with her to the place she now lived, but she felt bad about leaving it alone in a small apartment during the day, and she knew that her mother took better care of it than she did. When the daughter left, the white cat jumped up to the windowsill. It was waiting for the tabby to pass.

The tabby appeared just before sunset. After glancing up at the white cat, it would sit on the wall for a while, washing its face. Then it would walk farther along the wall and use the roof of the row house and the shed to jump down into the narrow alley, turning the corner by the small roadside shrine. Its routine was exactly the same every day, except when it was pouring rain or snowing.

One day, demolition work began on the vacant house, and the cat no longer passed by.

19

I feel like I want to see the places that someone else saw, he said; I like thinking about places I've been to once but I no longer know how to get to, or places that you can only access at certain times, I feel like there must be some way of visiting the places that exist only in people's memories

On the last Sunday in May, a novelist delivered a lecture at a community center.

After finishing her ninety-minute lecture, she stuck around for a short chat with the mayor, then left. As she stepped outside, an elderly woman approached and spoke to her. The zelkovas in the park where the community center was located were covered with tens of thousands of leaves, through which the sun, still high in the sky, filtered an iridescent light green.

The novelist felt that she had seen the elderly woman somewhere before. She was tiny, and looked like she must be over eighty. The elderly woman told the novelist that she was a distant relative of hers. She gave the name of the novelist's father's hometown, and the name of her second cousin, which the novelist recognized. It was the first time for the novelist to visit this part of the country, and she had never been told that she had relatives there.

As the elderly woman went on listing the names of relatives that she shared with the novelist, she pulled something out of a bag and showed it to her. It was a black-and-white photograph, the size of a business card. The photograph was torn and crumpled, but the image itself was distinct. It showed five children: the girls with bowl cuts, the boys with shaved heads. This is me, and this is your father, the elderly woman said. All the children in the photograph had similar faces, and the novelist had no idea who was who. The boy whom the elderly woman pointed out as her father was pulling a stern expression, perhaps wincing in the light, and the novelist thought that it sort of looked like her father, and sort of didn't. Oh, is it? the novelist said. It had been twenty years since her father's death. Goodness knows how many years ago this was taken, the old woman said. This is the only photograph that I have of him, but I shall give it to you. The woman had a genteel way of speaking, utterly different from the people from the fishing town where the novelist's father came from, and the novelist was unable to connect the person standing in front of her with her father's relatives. Keep well, the elderly woman said. Thank you very much, the novelist said, holding on to the photograph in something of a daze. She didn't like giving lectures, and her head felt a little numb afterward, so this sudden turn of events had thrown her slightly. When the elderly woman turned away, the novelist saw a young man behind her. The novelist wondered how long he'd been standing there. The young man bowed his head in her direction, so the novelist did the same. Then she watched the pair walk off, wondering if the boy was the woman's grandson, which would presumably make him a distant relative of hers as well.

A HUNDRED YEARS AND A DAY / *117*

After returning home, the novelist studied the photograph. The children in it were standing in front of a low stone wall, the branches of a pine tree behind them. Five years earlier the novelist's mother had also passed away, and she had grown distant from her father's relatives, so she couldn't think of anyone she could ask about the photograph or the woman who'd given it to her. She put it in a drawer where she kept her passport. Seven years later, the novelist suddenly fell ill and was rushed to hospital. She died without ever returning home.

A month after her death, the novelist's two daughters came to sort through her possessions. The older daughter lived abroad and hadn't made it over in time to attend her funeral. The younger daughter also lived far away and since moving had only seen her mother every two or three years. The novelist had divorced when the girls were still young. Her ex-husband came to the funeral, where he saw his daughters for the first time in a long while. He had no possessions in the novelist's house, and said that even if they came across anything of his, he didn't mind if they just disposed of it.

The girls called up a used bookstore they knew and took their mother's books there, and then set about sorting the remaining things into various piles. The clothes, the tableware, the things the girls had used when they were young—everything was scattered haphazardly around the small house, crammed into drawers and cupboards. The girls realized they could end up spending months and months going through everything individually and still not be done, so midway through they stopped

118 / TOMOKA SHIBASAKI

digging down to the bottom of each box and began assigning things to piles based on first impressions.

The familial bonds are quite weak among our relatives, aren't they, the older daughter said, as the two of them stood surrounded by towering piles of stuff. That's true, I don't think I've ever been to any kind of Buddhist memorial service. I guess a few years after we die there'll be nobody who remembers her, or this house. Maybe there'll still be people reading Mom's books, though. It's funny to think of her books on someone's shelves somewhere.

Because of the disarray of the novelist's possessions, and because their deadline was fast approaching, the two girls worked through the rooms and the closets without getting especially sentimental. As they were going through the drawers by the kitchen table that held a jumble of papers, electrical cords, cups, and so on, like everywhere else, they discovered a black and white photo. The small photo looked like it was from another era, taken before the novelist was born.

Who's this photo of, I wonder? the older daughter said. Goodness knows. Maybe Grandma or Grandpa? Or maybe it was part of her research for a book, the younger daughter said. In the years leading up to her death, the novelist had written several books about a town that had been bombed during the air raids. They had found old maps, photos, and photocopied documents relating to those works stashed in various places around the house.

It says Matsubara on the back, the younger daughter said, glancing at the back of the photo. Is that a place name, or a person's name? We don't have any relatives with that surname, do we?

It had been decided that the house would be sold to the next-door neighbors, who had been wanting to expand their property anyway, and the agreement was that they would clear it within a month. If she was some kind of literary master, these kinds of things would be displayed in the archives of her museum, one of the daughters said. But I'm guessing there's not going to be a museum. Doesn't she have any letters from famous people?

The two daughters sorted through clothes and tableware, and the mountains of paper, which there was far more of than anything else, getting covered in dust as they did. The novelist had written her novels on a computer, so there were no handwritten manuscripts. They came across some prepublication printouts and galley proofs of her own books, but most of the papers were flyers for events and films, maps and leaflets brought home from trips she'd taken, and various pamphlets—miscellaneous printed materials that were hard to categorize. An editor who had known the novelist for a long time visited the house the following day and helped to sort through the papers, reducing them to just one box, which it was decided the younger daughter would take with her. The black-and-white photo was put inside in a family photo album that the younger daughter also took home.

For five days, the two daughters stayed in their mother's house, going through her things. It was twenty years since the two of them had lived there. They slept in their old room on the second floor, which was the only part of

120 / TOMOKA SHIBASAKI

the house that hadn't been used by their mother as storage space and therefore remained uncluttered, but with so much dust flying around, they couldn't stop sneezing.

The first floor, where the novelist had spent most of her day, eating and working, fell in the shadow of the adjacent apartment building and stayed gloomy even during the daytime. The daughters retained a mental image of the afternoon sun shining into the first floor, as it had throughout the time they were living there, and in the now-altered space they struggled to sense the passing of time.

On the final day, a house clearance company came by, leaving the interior virtually empty, and the daughters turned the property over to the real estate agent. The older daughter got on a plane and returned overseas, and the younger daughter drove the five-hour journey home.

The younger daughter's partner took an interest in the photograph that the sisters had found in the chest of drawers. He asked if she had any clue as to who it might be. None at all, the younger daughter replied.

The following autumn, the younger daughter visited a seaside town to deliver a presentation at an academic society to which she belonged. Her partner came with her and explored the area. The town was close to the novelist's father's hometown, so they decided to make a stop there, too. The younger daughter hadn't visited the fishing village since she was five, and her memories of it were hazy. She walked around, unclear on where her grandfather's family had lived.

On a hill overlooking the fishing port, where there were far fewer boats than there had once been, houses were built so close to one another that their eaves practically touched. Alleys taking the form of staircases scaled the tiny gaps between them, branching off in all directions. The daughter's partner raised his voice in admiration at this unique sight, saying *woah*, that's incredible, and taking out his cellphone to take photographs. It seemed like a lot of the houses stood vacant, and the place was quiet—there was barely anyone in sight. A bald, burly man sat midway up one of the staircases. The younger daughter greeted him, telling him that her grandfather had been born around here, but the man said that he'd moved from a nearby town forty years ago, and didn't really know about anything further back in time. Showing him the photograph, the younger daughter asked if there was a place called Matsubara nearby, or if he knew anyone with that name? The bald man said he didn't know anyone called Matsubara, or any places with that name, but it was a word he was familiar with. It was what they called the pine trees that had been planted as a windbreak. There was one by the beach here, and one by the beach in the next town, and in the towns beyond as well.

Then, squinting at the photograph, the bald man said that he thought this might have been taken at the shrine, close to the top of this hill. There hadn't been anyone to take care of the shrine for a while, mind.

The daughter and her partner thanked the man, and took the stairs up the hill. There they saw a torii gate and a small shrine. The door to the shrine seemed like it hadn't been opened in a long time, and the wood of the torii had seen better days, but the shrine grounds were tidy and set off from the surrounding trees, so it seemed that someone was at least coming in to do some gardening. They compared the place to the photograph, but although there were similar-looking pine trees, there was no stone wall in sight. I guess you couldn't know just from looking at this photo where it was taken, could you? There aren't enough identifying features, the younger daughter and her partner said to one another.

Turning back to look at the path they'd climbed, they saw the sea peeking out between the gaps in the trees, and a section of the beach below. The sand beyond the dense vegetation was shining a hazy white, and the two stood staring at it for a while.

Just then someone came climbing up the hill. It was a child. They asked if the child lived here, and the child announced that they were the last child in the village. When they graduated, their school would close, and there would be no more village festivals. Is that so, I guess that's happening everywhere these days, as more and more people move to the cities, the younger daughter's partner said. Then they asked the child how to get to the beach. The child told them that you couldn't get to the beach from up here. There was no pathway from the village either. The beach was only accessible by sea—you had to go round the cape in a boat to get there. Then the child headed off down the other side of the hill. The daughter and her partner returned to the village, saying to one another that that must be why the beach was so beautiful, if people couldn't walk there and the only access was by sea, and that they would like to visit it one day.

Five years passed, and the last child became the last-ever student to graduate from that junior high school. The last child's family moved to a town in the mountains about an hour's drive away. It was a small town, but it had a hot spring and an art museum, and it was one of the venues for an annual art festival that had started up in that particular prefecture several years previously, which had brought more visitors to the area.

The last child graduated from high school and then, while working in a shop, volunteered as a visitor's guide for the art festival. That summer, like the summers before, artists came and built their installations around the hot spring and the old wooden houses there. One day, the last child went around looking at the artworks that were nearing completion. Peering into the vacated classroom of an elementary school that was being used as one of the venues, the last child saw houses and alleyways. The houses with tile roofs were so close that their eaves were touching, and alleys and staircases ran between them. They looked a lot like the houses in the seaside town where the last child had grown up. But they were meticulously constructed at a fifth of their actual size. A block of about ten houses sat there in the classroom, like a segment cut from something larger. The description of the work stated that this was a sculptural piece constructed entirely of wood, based on a place in a novel. The last child didn't recognize the name of the novel or the person who'd written it, and in any case, the place featured in the novel was an imaginary place, where time passed differently for different people.

There was no one else in the classroom. The windows were open and the last child could see the green paddy fields and the mountains beyond.

The last child crouched down and peered into the alley running between the wooden houses. It looked a lot like the alleyways that they knew from their childhood. They felt as though it was a path they'd been down before. As the last child was still staring down the passage, a cat ran across the end of the alleyway where the stone steps were. The last child gasped in surprise, and stood up. A cicada flew in through the window, attached itself to the wall, and began to screech.

20

Family Tree II

Around the time my maternal grandmother was born, there was a murder in her neighborhood. I had only just started school when I heard about it from her, and it came as a shock. But then, everything shocked me when I was a child. I've forgotten now why we were talking about it. I imagine we saw a report of a similar incident on the news or something.

My grandmother had grown up in a town where most of the population worked in one of the many factories by the estuary. Her father had moved there immediately after finishing junior high school to take up a job in a nearby shipbuilding factory. He'd told my grandmother that he'd lived in what had been called "workers' housing," which was actually a set of rickety wooden apartments crammed to bursting with young men. It was quite fun nonetheless, he said. Kids find a way of enjoying themselves wherever they end up, my grandmother commented, but hearing that as a kid myself, I worried that I'd be moved into apartments like that and made to work in a factory one day. I'd only ever seen my grandmother's father in a photograph.

My grandmother's father had met my grandmother's mother in that shipbuilding factory. My grandmother's mother joined the accounts department of the company after she'd graduated from commercial high school,

| 125

five years after my grandfather's father started working there. She'd grown up in that same town, and lived just across the river from the factory. She'd apparently told my grandmother's father that her reason for choosing it was precisely because it was so close. My grandmother didn't know the details about how they'd met. She said that, it being the olden days, the people around them had probably remarked on how they were similar in age and goaded them on until they agreed to marry, which in turn made me worry that I was going to be made to marry someone because they were similar in age to me.

My grandmother's parents had married young and lived in a wooden row house, one station along from the factory. It was a small house, with just one room on the first floor and one on the second, but everywhere was like that at the time. Several other young couples lived in the same line of row houses. You'd hear the sound of babies screaming, and there were lots of kids playing in the alley that ran in back. After about a year they gave birth to a daughter—my grandmother—but for a long time they couldn't settle on a name for her. My grandmother's mother's parents weren't satisfied with the name they came up with, saying the stroke count for the kanji wasn't auspicious. One night, when the deadline by which they needed to register the new birth was growing near, my grandmother's mother was awake in the middle of the night feeding her newborn daughter, when she heard the sound of something breaking. It was a noise like she'd never heard before, a mixture of glass shattering and something hard smashing to pieces. Then it fell quiet.

The following day, a number of police showed up at the row house behind theirs. The neighbors told them that the husband had been killed. There had been rumors circulating that the man was a gambler and had worked up debts, and now the yakuza had come for him. You heard of that sort of thing a lot back then, her grandmother said, and I had the thought that my grandmother had been born into a world where everything was terrifying.

After that, my grandmother's mother frequently ran into the wife of the murdered man at the market. She was a quiet type with a pleasant manner. Looking at my grandmother in her mother's arms, the woman commented that the baby looked exactly like her father. My grandmother's mother had told my grandmother that she remembered the occasion well, because everyone else said how much the girl took after her mother.

My grandmother's mother turned ninety-five last month.

21

Mizushima is injured in a traffic accident and is in hospital for a while, but he is left with no permanent physical damage; seven years later, when his memories of the accident are fading, he bumps into Yokota, who had been driving the car that caused the accident, while on a work trip to Tokyo

In the second year of his first job, Mizushima was in a traffic accident. He was on his way back from a camping trip with university friends. Eleven of them had traveled in three cars, staying two nights in a campground near a ravine.

On the way home, they'd played rock paper scissors to decide who should go in what car on the way home. The car that Mizushima ended up in that day was driven by Yokota. It was a small sky-blue car that he'd just bought. Mizushima and Yokota had been out drinking a few times with mutual friends, but they weren't close.

The day was getting dark, and there was a sudden downpour. The road that laced through the foothills of the mountain twisted gently. The sky-blue car, swerving to avoid an oncoming truck that had crossed the center line, skidded and crashed into a traffic light pole, then toppled into a paddy field.

All three passengers were wearing seatbelts, and neither vehicle had been going that fast, but when people saw the car, a third of which had been crushed, they said it was a miracle that they'd made it out alive.

It was three months after the accident that Mizushima first saw a photo of the car. He'd been in the passenger seat, on the side that crashed into the traffic light, and he'd broken bones in his hips and legs. For those first three months in hospital, he could barely move. It was around that long, too, before he saw Yokota and the person who'd been in the back seat, since they'd been taken to a different hospital.

Aside from a slight numbness in his left leg, Mizushima didn't experience any lasting effects from the crash. He was able to return to work almost immediately after being discharged from hospital. The company he worked for was small, and he'd landed the job through a family connection, so the people at his workplace had told him that he should take his time recovering, and not worry about hurrying back.

The person sitting in the back seat, whose injuries had only been minor, was discharged from the hospital after a week, and he was able to return to his job in hospitality. Mizushima heard afterward that Yokota, who'd been working for a company in Tokyo, had quit his job. Yokota had broken his shoulder and had ten stitches in his forehead, but physically, he'd recovered just fine. The problem was that he was working in sales, in a job that required him to drive, which he could no longer do after the accident. Mizushima heard all this from a friend who was close to Yokota. He heard, also, that Yokota was now working on contract, paid by the hour.

Yokota's parents visited Mizushima in their son's place and apologized for what had happened, discussing the matter of the hospital fees with Mizushima's parents. When Mizushima asked how Yokota was, they said that he was doing well, but was so busy that he rarely picked up when they called him.

Yokota wouldn't pick up when Mizushima tried to get in touch with him, either. Mizushima figured that maybe he didn't want to be reminded of the accident. For a while, Mizushima himself had struggled to get in a car, particularly in the passenger seat. He avoided buses too, where possible. Sometimes, when it was dusk and it began to rain, flashes would come back to him with eerie vividness: of the oncoming truck's headlights, or the way they'd lit up the raindrops and the broken glass. Each time this happened, Mizushima would find himself unable to move for a while.

It was the following summer that he heard from a different friend, who'd been in the same year at university and was now working in Tokyo, that he'd bumped into Yokota and he'd seemed fine. After that, Mizushima didn't hear any more about him. He saw less and less of his university friends, and never thought to make an effort to get in touch with Yokota, who he'd never been that close to in the first place.

Seven years passed and Mizushima, although he couldn't drive himself, no longer had any difficulty getting into a car. Sometimes the memory of the crash would come rushing back to him, when he caught sight of his scars in the bath, or saw news of a traffic accident on the

TV, but all was going well at work, and he and the person he'd been dating for three years were contemplating marriage. When he went to Tokyo for work, he didn't think about Yokota.

One day, Mizushima was on one such business trip to Tokyo. He'd finished work for the day and was drinking alone in an izakaya near a client's office. His eyes landed on the back of someone sitting at a table nearby. The man's slumped posture somehow looked familiar. When the person stood up, Mizushima's conviction grew. Yokota! he called out.

Oh, hi, Yokota replied, as if they'd seen each other only yesterday. Yokota had been getting up to go, but at Mizushima's suggestion he took the seat beside him, and Mizushima ordered them each a beer.

Yokota told Mizushima that he now had a permanent job in the accounts department for a small company, that he wasn't exactly comfortably off but he was getting by. Mizushima told him that he had largely forgotten about the accident, that sometimes he'd remember it as though it were happening all over again, but everything was fine with him physically, and if Yokota was holding onto any guilt about causing the accident, then he wanted him to let go of it.

Having listened to this in silence, Yokota told Mizushima that he didn't remember anything about the accident. When Mizushima reminded him that they'd spoken about it when Yokota had come to visit him in hospital, he said that at that point, he'd felt like he remembered it, but that after a while, all of his memories from around that time had vanished. He barely remembered anything from his student days, either. When Mizushima had called out to him, he felt as if he recognized his face and so he'd responded, but he hadn't really known who he was. He'd sat down with him, figuring that as they were talking it'd come back to him. He was really and truly sorry about the accident. As Yokota said all this, there was something not quite right about his demeanor—as if he wasn't all there, as if he were just leasing out somebody else's body.

When Mizushima remarked that it must be hard living in Tokyo, far from his family and without many acquaintances, and then reiterated that he didn't have any lasting damage from the accident and he really didn't want it to weigh on Yokota's consciousness, Yokota seemed to take in what he was saying. He mumbled, as if to himself, that he found it easier being here. For a long time, he said, he'd always wanted to become someone else other than himself, which was maybe why his memories had disappeared.

Mizushima didn't know how to respond to this. He tried joking that he'd be sad if Yokota forgot about him entirely, but Yokota only nodded, absently.

After returning home, Mizushima told his friends that he'd run into Yokota. One of his friends said that he was fairly sure Yokota wasn't in Tokyo. He and his parents had moved back to their hometown, the friend told him. He was doing really well, he was married now and had kids. The friend laughed and said, that must have been someone else in Tokyo, who looked like him. I mean, he said he had no memory, he was probably just going along with what you said, no?

Now this was put to him, it struck Mizushima that the Yokota he'd met in the Tokyo izakaya had, in fact, just repeated what he himself had volunteered about the accident and their university days. Was it possible that it hadn't actually been Yokota? Mizushima asked his friend to get Yokota's contact details. He couldn't get through to him on the phone, so he wrote a letter to the address in the far-off town, but received no reply.

Mizushima got married and had two children. He bought a small house. His kids pleaded with him to go camping during the summer vacation. By now he could drive, but he didn't feel like going camping. Before he knew it, his children had found jobs and left home.

After several years, one of his university friends who'd been on that camping trip opened a soba restaurant, and Mizushima was invited to the launch party. The restaurant was surprisingly chic, and the soba they served was genuinely tasty. His friends looked different—their faces and bodies had aged—but they remembered the old days in surprising detail, and spoke enthusiastically about the past.

Feeling tired from all the talking, Mizushima sat down at the end of a big table in the center of the restaurant and drank a beer. The man sitting next to him was also drinking beer by himself, so Mizushima poured him a glass, then asked him where he knew the owner from. He's a friend from my university days, the man said. But I got injured in a car accident, and don't remember anything from that time. My memories from after that time are sketchy as well.

Mizushima looked into the man's face and hesitated before saying, Yokota? That's right, the man nodded. He looked both like and unlike the Yokota that Mizushima had once known.

22

**A man opens a cafe in a shopping arcade,
dreaming that it will become like the jazz cafe
he used to frequent as a student; the cafe stays
open for nearly thirty years, then closes down**

The cafe stood on the third corner of the old shopping arcade.

The building itself was pretty ramshackle, and in the showcase outside, the plastic models of cream soda, pancakes, sandwiches, and so on had faded and acquired a layer of dust. The door and outside wall were plastered with numerous little boards depicting menu items. Coffee in a plain cup and saucer, curry and rice with a serving of fukujinzuke pickles on the side, shaved ice in the summer and azuki bean porridge in the winter. The simple illustrations, which could hardly be called accomplished, were drawn by the cafe owner in thick marker pen. The prices were written in red.

Most days, mornings brought a series of two or three elderly men at a time, who would spread out their sports papers—newspapers that featured a range of sports, entertainment, and celebrity news. Come lunchtime, the space would grow lively with the sound of women talking.

The dilapidated old cafe had once been new. When it first opened, the plastic models of food were vividly colored, and the sign above the door with the coffee company logo lit up as it was supposed to. The cafe's owner had been young, too. Or, more accurately, he had been approaching forty. He'd just quit his job at an office supplies company, where he'd worked for almost two decades, and started up the cafe of his dreams.

The cafe was modeled on one he had frequented back in his student days in Tokyo. Positioned midway between the station and the university, the cafe played jazz, and students who were into music and films would sit in there for hours. Its wood-paneled walls had turned a caramel color and the tables were riddled with scratches. A jumble of magazines and works of foreign literature filled the shelves. In his student days, the owner had stopped in at the cafe at least twice a week. He'd fallen for a girl working there, but graduated and left town without ever telling her of his feelings.

When he decided to leave his office job, he returned to the place he grew up and opened his cafe in the shopping arcade outside the station, which he'd passed through every day until he finished high school. At busy times his wife, a former classmate of his, helped him out. People from his year at school who'd remained in the area came by, sometimes bringing their friends, and as a result, the business got off to a reasonable start.

The area was one where few people attended university. Most of the owner's junior high school classmates had gone on to work in factories along the coast or taken over their family businesses. There was a dignity about these people, who seemed so well suited to their jobs in the dried goods shop or the ironmonger in the arcade or one of the small factories in the area. They spoke of the

A HUNDRED YEARS AND A DAY / *137*

cafe owner, who'd gone to university and had a taste for European films and jazz, as something of an oddball.

The owner's father would complain to those around him that he'd sent his son off to university only to have him wind up running a cafe. With scorn, he would describe his son's new venture as part of the "water trade"—a general term for the entertainment business, including its less reputable parts. "Yes," his son would counter, smiling, "the water we're using is top quality, we're doing a great water trade."

The owner's father had died ten years previously, without once visiting his son's cafe. He'd even avoided passing in front of it. He'd been hospitalized for a year before his death, and during that time the owner went back and forth between the cafe and his father's bedside. His two children found jobs and moved to more convenient locations. His wife started volunteering as a conversation partner for local elderly people.

The cafe had strayed far from the owner's original vision. To suit his customers, it was now sports papers and baseball manga that lined the shelves. Told that the cafe's exterior wasn't very approachable, not the sort of place that someone ventured into off the street, he began out of desperation to draw pictures of coffee and curry on bits of board, which soon became a hit with the locals. He'd made more and more of these boards, sticking them up outside, until before long the cafe was featured on the local news channel as a "quirky spot," and that description stuck. Somehow, he became closer with his old schoolmates, whom he'd found hard to get along with when he was younger. It was actually quite fun running this kind of cafe, even if it wasn't what he'd initially intended, he'd think to himself. The one thing that hadn't changed was his commitment to playing music he liked, although now he played CDs, not records.

Over half the shops in the arcade eventually closed down. He was often reminded of a term he'd heard in a rakugo performance, back when he was young: shimotaya, or ex-shop. This arcade was lined with shimotaya, which were now used as houses. The older locals who frequented the cafe would moan about the situation, putting it down to the fact that young people these days wouldn't come to somewhere so unexciting. Another reason the arcade had gone to seed, though, was that many landlords didn't want to rent out their properties as shops, thinking it was more trouble than it was worth. In any case, the average age of his customers had certainly risen.

The arcade had been welcomed with open arms when it was first built, but now the awning made the street feel dingy and deserted even during the day. For a long time, the café with all the pictures outside served as a landmark in navigating the space.

Another decade passed, and the old cafe closed down.

At this time, the cafe near the university in Tokyo that the owner used to frequent was still in business. A woman who'd worked there part-time as a student took over the business at the age of twenty-seven. The previous owner had worked nonstop in the cafe until he was eighty-two, when he finally made the decision to take it easy and listen to his records at home in the suburbs.

A HUNDRED YEARS AND A DAY / *139*

The new owner didn't alter the place at all. She kept the battered walls, the bookshelves by the window, the chairs with ripped cushions, and the menu exactly as they were. Even the torn poster on the wall stayed put. It was a student band poster from long before her time. She had once asked the former owner what the band members were up to now. Yeah, I wonder, he had replied, with little interest. Did they come here often, the young woman had followed up. I guess they must have, if the poster's up on the wall. It seemed the former owner's memory was growing dim. She supposed that if every year brought an influx of new students, and that a similar number would leave, and that process was repeated for decades, then it stood to reason that you wouldn't remember them all. With this thought, the young owner didn't ask any more questions. The former owner spoke very rarely about the past. He just brewed coffee and made toast in silence, playing his records, day in, day out.

When the former owner left, he took his records home with him, so the sole thing that did change about the cafe was the music.

The young owner was into music. Her taste spanned diverse genres, from many different countries and time periods, so the cafe now played a real range of tunes.

As she stood behind the counter surveying the floor, it often struck the new owner that the space seemed entirely different depending on what music was playing. Nothing had changed, and yet those same walls that had been there for decades seemed to take on different colors. Time after time, the owner experienced how music, invisible to the eye, would spread through the air, changing everything about the place.

One hot summer evening, she put on some Kawachi Ondo, a type of folk music from the Osaka area. A friend whom she'd been going to concerts and festivals with since her student days had recommended a particular song to her.

She had neither a CD nor a record of said song, so she played the video on her smartphone, which she hooked up to the speakers. She'd grown up in an apartment in the city center, and, never having taken part in the traditional Bon Odori dance when Kawachi Ondo was played, the rhythm and the voices were utterly new to her. It was energetic yet laid-back, the kind of music that instantly made you want to get up and move.

As she dried the plates behind the counter, she found her feet tapping to the rhythm, her body moving. Looking up, she saw that the customers at the table directly in front of her were jiggling their shoulders. The pair of students by the window who, if she recalled correctly, were in a band that used African percussion instruments, started drumming on the table. The student next to them began clapping on the offbeats.

As the owner watched wide-eyed, the students' movements grew more pronounced, and in time they got up and started to dance. As if pulled in by the momentum, the people at the table in front of them also stood up. Then the one next to them.

The customers danced in the narrow spaces between the tables, each in their own way. The owner guessed that this wasn't how you were supposed to dance to Kawachi Ondo, but the music flowing from the speakers gave their separate movements a wonderful rolling motion that seemed to express a single consciousness. The cafe was buzzing.

This, the young owner thought to herself, this is what I wanted to do.

23

Growing up, two brothers are often told how close they are; the older brother moves away to study; the younger takes up the guitar and becomes famous; on a TV in an izakaya, the older brother sees his younger brother for the first time in ages

There were two brothers, two years apart, who were very close.

At least, the people who knew them would say that they were very close, said it often in fact, but the boys themselves didn't especially feel that way. As kids they fought a lot. They'd punch and kick and bite each other, and sometimes they actually injured each other. When the younger of the boys was about ten he threw a bike at his older brother, who ended up with five stitches on his arm. That got them into serious trouble with their parents, and from that point on there were fewer scuffles.

The reason people often remarked on how close the two boys were was doubtless that they were always together. The boys' parents worked at the grandfather's factory, so the earliest they got home in the evening was seven, and some days they weren't back until nine or ten in the evening. Their mother would return to the house at lunchtime and prepare the boys' dinner, so it would be waiting when they got home. In busier periods, though, that was hard to manage, and instead the boys would head out to a local soba shop or Chinese restaurant, clutching the 1,000-yen note their mother had left them. On days when she didn't leave any money, the older of the two would make a simple meal like yakisoba.

In part because the younger brother had asthma, and didn't especially like being outdoors, the two spent a lot of time inside. They would watch TV, or take it in turns to read the dozens of volumes of manga they borrowed from one of their classmates, who had an extensive collection.

The older brother performed well at school. He wasn't exceptionally studious, but he liked researching things and reading about subjects that interested him, and he found lessons engaging. He was fairly athletic as well, and sometimes when he missed school, girls from his class would bring him notes, and chat with him before heading off home.

The younger brother disliked anything related to schoolwork. For a long time he found it hard to accept that a line of letters strung together actually meant anything. Numbers were even more difficult. To him they just looked like little diagrams, or patterns. He wasn't any good at sports, and wasn't gifted at maintaining conversations, either. His parents worried about him, and were forever telling his older brother to keep an eye out for him, to help him when he could.

From the younger brother's perspective, though, his parents' attitude felt like a rejection of who he was, a sign that they didn't believe him capable of anything, and that left him angry. His brother was the only person who really listened to him when he talked about the minutiae of a particular TV program or manga series, and he appreciated it when his brother looked out for him, too. But his relatives, and the people from the neighborhood, were always finding ways of comparing him with his brother, saying, "And to think the older one is so good at everything!" For this reason, the boy would occasionally lash out at his brother when they were in public.

To the older boy, it felt as though their parents were completely focused on his younger brother. Whether he performed well in tests, or got picked for the relay team for sports day, his parents reacted without surprise, as if such things were expected of him. This gave rise to conflicted feelings in him. He was aware that his relatives and neighbors would say that all he ever did was study, that he was a goody two-shoes. He also knew that his parents, who hoped that he would eventually take over the family factory, didn't want him to go away to university or to study a subject that wasn't practical in nature.

When the younger brother started junior high school, his homeroom teacher invited him to join the guitar club he ran, which was short on members. The boy had never touched an instrument before, but he had fast fingers and perhaps something of a natural aptitude, for he made rapid progress. His ability soon overtook that of the teacher himself, who had been in a fairly popular rock band when he was younger, and at the end of the second year, the boy won second prize in a contest.

The boys' parents were delighted to find that their younger son, whose future had been such a concern, had an unexpected talent, the discovery of which seemed to have given him a new lease of confidence. When people from the neighborhood congratulated him or eyed him enviously, the parents would happily say that they'd known from a young age that there was something special about him.

While the younger brother was being showered with attention, the older brother, now in high school, devoted himself to his studies. His passion was astronomy. Ever since visiting the local planetarium as a small child with a friend's family, and being overwhelmed by that glimpse of outer space, twinkling with so many points of light it almost made him nauseous, he'd dreamed of studying the distant stars. Over and over he would watch clips of astronauts standing inside their spaceships and explaining their scientific experiments, thinking that that was what he wanted to do when he grew up. He stopped hanging out so much with his classmates, spending his time instead either in the school or the public library, studying for his university exams. His hard work paid off, and he went on to study at a national university in a far-off, rural part of the country. You could see the stars clearly there, unlike the industrial district where he'd grown up, and the university was home to the academic who'd written one of his most beloved books.

His parents opposed the move at first, but seeing that the boy's mind was set, they eventually gave in. It helped that with the long-standing economic downturn, the future of the factory wasn't looking so bright, and they were no longer sure if it was such a good idea to have their son take over. The boy looked into scholarships and living costs, and presented them with a written proposal, detailing how much he could cover if he took a part-time job.

The day the older brother left for university, the younger had band practice, and he didn't come to see him off. The older brother was fine with that. He found that living in a new place where he didn't know anybody suited him. At university he wasn't anybody's son, or anyone's older brother. He could see the stars, and nobody minded if he spent all day every day studying. Just as he'd anticipated, the academic who had written his favorite book was a capable, devoted teacher, and the boy enjoyed their conversations. He got a part-time job in the cram school by the station, and that covered most of his living expenses.

The younger brother began seeing an older woman he met at a gig. The woman was very beautiful, and a talented drummer, something of a local celebrity. The boy moved into her apartment, and his most blissful moments were those he spent lying in the hammock on her balcony, strumming his guitar.

The two brothers fell out of touch. As a response to his childhood, the younger brother was full of a stubborn determination to prove that he could get by in life without his older brother, and the fact that he was making money and being showered with applause and praise was a source of satisfaction to him.

The older brother thought less and less about his family and the place he'd grown up. Then one evening, shortly after beginning his PhD, he saw his brother on the TV in the izakaya where he'd gone for a drink with some other students from his research lab. It was a music program, introducing up-and-coming bands. His brother looked cool, he thought, playing the guitar on television like that. In a way, he seemed totally different from the boy he'd known, but he felt proud of him. Nobody in the izakaya knew it was his brother, though, and he didn't say anything.

The older brother took a job as a teaching assistant at the university and continued his research. One evening a woman showed up unexpectedly at his apartment. It was the end of fall, and the temperature plummeted in the evenings.

His brother had gone missing, the woman told him. It was the beautiful drummer that his brother had been living with for some time. She wore a plain black dress, but even so there was an air of glamour about her that stood out a mile in this rural town. He invited her into his apartment, but she refused, and stayed standing on his doorstep. She told him that his brother had left her apartment about two weeks ago, and she hadn't heard from him since. There had been times in the past when he'd disappeared for a couple of days, but he'd never been gone for anything like this long. He was in a period of preparation before work started in earnest on the next album, so it was possible he'd decided to take a holiday, but still, she was concerned. She mentioned that he'd spoken about his older brother often, which came as a surprise. Apparently he used to say that, quite unlike himself, his older brother was kind and generally good at everything, the source of much pride. The woman said that she'd been visiting a nearby town on tour with her band, and had decided to try this address, which she'd found in the younger brother's diary. The older brother had no idea why his younger brother would keep his address in his diary, when the two had never written, let alone visited each other.

The woman asked him not to mention anything about the disappearance to his parents. The younger brother was always saying that he didn't want to cause them any trouble, she said. Like everything else the woman said, he found this description impossible to connect up with the brother that he had known.

After the woman went home, he tried phoning his brother, but there was no answer. He called his parents, probing subtly for information, but they didn't seem to know anything. The factory was cutting back its workforce, and his parents were exhausted.

It was about three months later that the woman called him. The younger brother had returned home a little while ago, she said. It turned out that he'd been off with someone he'd been seeing on the side, but the two of them had decided to give things another go. Oh I see, said the older brother. Well, please say hello to him from me, and with that he put down the phone.

After that, a letter arrived from his younger brother. The younger brother didn't mention women at all, talking instead about his trips to Vietnam and Thailand. Attached to the letter were two very touristy postcards.

A little while later, the older brother heard the younger brother's latest single on the radio. Of everything he'd heard by him so far, this was the song he liked the best.

24

Yamamoto found a rooftop apartment to live in, then moved to another rooftop apartment with a big balcony, then moved into yet another apartment; at one time there was a woman around, at another time he spoke with his neighbor

When it came to finding a place to live, Yamamoto specifically looked for apartments that were like huts perched on a rooftop, or that had big balconies.

His dream apartment was one he'd seen on TV as a kid, where a detective had lived. He'd decided back then that when he grew up, he'd live in a place like that. It was about the only thing that Yamamoto had dreamed of doing when he was an adult that he'd actually managed to make a reality.

There were a surprising number of rooftop-hut apartments and apartments with big balconies out there. Around the time Yamamoto first began living alone, he got off at a station that caught his attention for some reason, and inquired at a local real estate office about such properties, only to be shown three places that matched his criteria. Now, with a quick online search, he could find any number of them immediately. The sticking point was that the buildings they were in tended to be old, and sometimes they were on the fourth or fifth floor, without any elevator. That was partly the reason why there were a lot of those kinds of places without tenants.

The first apartment he lived in was truly like a hut. It was a prefab cabin perched on the roof of a four-story building in front of the station. Tenants living on the lower floors and trainees from the barber that was at street level came up to the roof to dry their towels, and men from a slightly dubious health food company on the third floor headed there to smoke, so Yamamoto's dream of stringing up a hammock and relaxing there didn't come to pass. The real estate agent told him that the hut, which had a tiny kitchen and small bathroom of its own, had been built by the owner of the building, who had previously lived on the fourth floor, as a place for his son to study for his entrance exams. As if in proof of this, there was a hole in the wall at one of the corners. Yamamoto figured that the kid must have kicked it or hit it with a baseball bat or something. He placed a cardboard box in front of it. He'd been offered very cheap rent on the condition that he didn't mind the hole going unfixed. Yamamoto commuted from that apartment to the mail-order office machinery company where he'd found a job straight out of university. It was a single twenty-minute train ride away.

Having people lurking around directly outside his window day and night left him feeling unsettled, but after a while, he found himself on speaking terms with a few of them—in particular, with the part-time teachers from the cram school on the second-floor. In the past, cram-school teachers had mostly been students themselves, but now there were more and more who stayed on in their roles after graduating, unable to find other work. One of them was a tall guy who'd studied quantum mechanics at university, who told Yamamoto that there was an apartment of the kind he was looking for in a building owned by someone he knew. When Yamamoto checked out the location, it turned out to be easy to get to from his work. Of late, it was increasingly common for the door to his apartment, which anybody could access from the roof, to be knocked on or opened in the middle of the night, and so he decided to move.

His second apartment was right by the river—although the view it offered wasn't tranquil grassy banks, but a canal close to the industrial district. He saw mostly lead-colored water, gray concrete, and brown rust. It was an unusual building, with a line of apartments spanning its high-ceilinged second floor. The room at the end had a roof terrace. The terrace was really just a section of concrete roof that had been left over, but it was 13 square meters, about the same area as the apartment itself. Yamamoto placed a simple deckchair on it. From there he had a good view of the barges loaded with gravel traveling up the canal. Yet the absence of buildings above it to block the sun meant it was hot in summer, and the wind coming off the river made it chilly in winter.

Not many people lived in the neighborhood. The building was surrounded by warehouses and offices whose function remained somewhat obscure, and at night and on the weekends it seemed as though it had been forgotten by the world. He barely ever saw the other tenants. One Sunday when there was no sign of anyone around, he was watching the barges come and go on the river from the terrace when he found himself wondering if he'd died, and was now drifting around in another era of history.

He lived there for two years, but began to long for somewhere with a bit more life. The next place he moved to was in the center of the city, in a gap between taller buildings. He found it on a real estate website. The apartment sat on the roof of a five-story building, but didn't feel that way—instead, it felt like being at the bottom of a hole. On three of its sides it was surrounded by the windowless walls of taller buildings, while on the fourth, the sound barrier for the highway loomed right up close.

It's on a roof but it's got no view at all, was Yamamoto's thought when he first saw it. Yet his original motivation for being on a roof wasn't the scenery, but how it reminded him of the place the TV detective had lived, and he actually found the seediness of it, and the feeling of being tucked away like that right in the heart of the city, quite exciting. On the roof of the next building along was a huge sign facing the highway. He liked watching the workers who came from time to time to change the message on the billboard.

For a while, a woman lived with him in that apartment. She was a friend of a friend, and he'd met her several times when he went out for drinks with a group. The fourth time they went out drinking, he brought her back to his apartment. I wish I lived somewhere like this, I'm jealous, she said, and began leaving more and more of her stuff there. The woman worked at a big company everybody had heard of, and could have afforded an expensive apartment in a beautiful high-rise, but seemed fond of this grotto-like place never touched by the sun's rays. The woman was delighted when Yamamoto cooked for her, and seeing her delighted face also made Yamamoto happy.

After a year, Yamamoto arrived home one day to find the woman gone. They'd gotten into a fight a little while back over something silly, but he'd not suspected that she'd leave. All of the things that she'd brought with her had disappeared. On the table was a short note together with the keys to the car that the woman drove, which Yamamoto had always said how much he liked. When he used the map she'd drawn to get to the parking lot, the small yellow car was parked there.

At the end of that year, Yamamoto moved again to a different place. It was a two-room apartment on the top floor of a four-story building, and both rooms led onto the balcony. The balcony was three times the area of the apartment itself.

The balcony was surrounded by railings, giving him a perfect view of the next balcony along. He often saw his neighbor there. He was convinced his neighbor was far older, but it turned out that they were the same age. The neighbor was a large man with a laid-back demeanor. Neither he nor Yamamoto minded when both of them were out on the balcony at the same time. Even when Yamamoto would bring a friend round, and the two of them drank beer on the balcony and made a bit of a noise, the neighbor would only ever say, looks like fun. He didn't seem to mind at all, but neither did he join in with them.

One time, Yamamoto was dozing on a deckchair he'd

bought in a big-box store when, unusually, his neighbor started a conversation with him over the balcony railings.

There's something I've been wondering . . .

Yes?

Can you see that balcony? Second from the right, third from the top.

The neighbor pointed to an apartment building on the other side of the main road. It was a medium-sized brown-tile building, ever so regular looking. The neighbor was indicating the balcony on the fifth floor.

There's someone in there who's always looking this way. Look, they're resting their arms on the railing now.

Yamamoto squinted but he couldn't make out the person in question.

They must have so much time on their hands. What are they doing, do you think?

Saying this, the neighbor spread himself out on his blue vinyl sheet. He would sometimes lie practically naked in the middle of the balcony. Yamamoto would worry that he'd get heatstroke.

The weather grew colder, and just as Yamamoto was thinking that he hadn't seen his neighbor in a while, he realized that his room was empty. He must have moved out without Yamamoto noticing.

Yamamoto looked at the balcony of the brown-tile building that his neighbor had pointed out to him. As he was watching, a figure emerged from inside. A fat man was going in and out. He couldn't be sure from so far away, but the man looked a lot like his neighbor. It seemed to him that the man looked toward him and waved.

Yamamoto liked that apartment, but it was announced that the strip of buildings it was a part of was being redeveloped and it would be demolished, so he took the eviction payment and moved out.

His next apartment was right by the railway tracks, and was very noisy. He lived there for two years.

After that, Yamamoto quit his job and moved back to the town on the Japan Sea coast where his parents lived. He drove there in the small yellow car. His parents died one after the other and he inherited their two-story forty-year-old house. It was a fairly standard house of the kind built by a real estate developer, and sold together with the land. Yamamoto had found a job in a local office machinery company and was getting accustomed to life there, so he decided to add a balcony onto the house. It actually had a balcony already, but only a narrow one, just wide enough for a laundry rack. It seemed to him that if he only had a big balcony, he'd feel like his life was going the way he wanted it to.

The second floor was only half the area of the first floor, so he decided to create as big a balcony as he could on that section of first-floor roof. He bought the necessary materials from the home improvement store, and constructed the balcony little by little, all by himself. Just as he was about to finish it, Yamamoto fell from the roof and broke his shoulder. He paused his building work for a little while then, but resumed it again the following spring. Then he got a dog.

25

Daughter Tales III

"I heard this from a colleague where I used to work," the younger daughter began. She was sitting by the window in a cafe.

"At the place they were working before—I'm pretty sure it was a construction company—there was this guy who stopped coming into work, out of the blue."

"Wait, is this a scary story?" the daughter's older sister asked.

"Just listen! It was a young guy from the accounts department, and he rang in one day to say he was going to be late, and then from that point on he just stopped coming into work. He wouldn't pick up the phone when they called him, so they called his parents who he'd put down as his emergency contacts, and his parents said that he was at home, that there was no need to worry. So the boss was like, well, it's not just that we're worried, he's getting behind with his work, it's causing lots of problems, and we have some questions for him, if he's going to take time off, then he needs to go through the usual procedures. But apparently the parents didn't really seem to get it. Until that point he'd been a very normal employee, and hadn't acted weird or anything. Sometimes he'd pulled a face when people questioned him about a document he'd made or asked him to redo something, but that was about it."

"Ahh, there's someone like that at my work too, as soon as they get criticized about anything, they take the whole day off."

"So they'd heard from his parents that he wasn't coming in, but it got to ten days, and then two weeks, and his paid holidays were running out, so his boss went along with one of his colleagues to his apartment, but nobody answered the door. So they went round to his parents' house, which was nearby, and it was empty. The neighbor told them that the parents had moved out."

"Is this gonna be a scary story?"

"And by now they couldn't get through to the parents, either, so they discussed whether they should file a missing person's report or get the landlord to open the door to the guy's apartment, but then the next day the guy showed up at work, acting like nothing had happened. He was like, I wasn't feeling well but I'm better now, and all this. Of course they asked what was going on with his parents' house, but he said that his parents had bought an apartment and had moved the previous day. Whatever questions they asked, he'd give that kind of response, and he was going about his work normally again, so that even the people from his department got used to the situation after a while, or else just forgot about it. And then after five years, he filed the paperwork to say that he'd got married. Out of the blue. There was no ceremony or anything: he just reported it. The boss was like, you've not told us anything about it up until now, when did this all come about, and the guy said, she helped me out and supported me back when I was off work ages ago, when my parents died suddenly in an accident and I was really struggling, at which the boss was like, what, we never heard about your parents dying, I'm pretty sure back then you said they'd moved, and the guy goes, back then I was in too much pain and I couldn't tell anybody about it. Do you think that can actually be true?"

"I mean, who knows!"

"When they asked him about it in more detail, it seemed as though it was true that his parents had bought an apartment and moved, but then immediately after that, they'd had a car accident while they were visiting their hometown, and there'd been a short article about it in the paper and everything—in other words, as far as they looked into it, his story seemed to check out. And the guy continued to do well at work, and his communication skills got better and stuff. But the person who told me about it said that the story had stuck with them all this time, and several years after leaving the company, when they asked a former colleague how the guy was doing, they'd said that he was working hard and had become head of their section, and that there were fewer people around now who knew about what had happened in the past, and there was talk of him being promoted to department head, but then he was caught out for tax evasion on money he'd made from currency trading, and so the general conclusion was that he was a weirdo after all. Although they said that it didn't seem like he was making lots of money from investments."

"You know that thing that was in the magazines about the woman who escaped overseas with a huge fortune she'd made through an investment scandal? She lived really near where we were living when I was young. She was the mom of the friend of a junior colleague of a former classmate of mine, and apparently never seemed like the kind of person to do something like that. That junior colleague is working in a prefectural office somewhere in Kyushu, and apparently she's running for election soon."

The older sister sitting opposite began speaking of the junior colleague, and they both ordered another coffee.

26

In an international airport were some female students waiting for their flight to begin boarding, a married couple with a baby, and a woman who had once been seen off there by her father; before it became an international airport, a man flew a plane from there

Some female students were chatting in the airport. They still had an hour until their flight, which would take them back home after a ten-day holiday. On said holiday, they'd visited four cities in two countries. It was fun, wasn't it, said one of the students. Which place did you like best? a different student asked. The food in that cafe by the port was so good, another said.

The airport terminal was long and narrow. It would have taken almost an hour to walk from one end to the other. There was a line of extremely long moving walkways. Shuttle carts motored around, deftly evading the crowds, and an endless string of announcements filled the air. One of the girls watched the airplanes taking off on the other side of the enormous glass wall. A plane would lift off and then, after a pause, another would do exactly the same. From behind the glass, nothing could be heard. That's weird, the girl thought to herself, in reality it must be so phenomenally loud. Weird to think that just a bit of glass stopped you from hearing a thing. The airplanes leapt lightly into the air, then disappeared into the white clouds, as though they were part of a mechanism in a diorama. She could hardly believe that in no time, they themselves would board a plane like that and jet off into the sky in the same way. That for over ten hours they would fly continuously across that vast distance.

Where do you want to go next? Hey, are you there?

At the sound of her friends' insistent voices, the girl snapped back to herself. Hmm, well, we were by the sea a lot for this one, so maybe the desert next time? Her friends laughed at her answer. The desert!? So extreme! That's a bit simplistic, isn't it, to say we've done the sea now so next is the desert? The girl who wanted to go to the desert didn't know why they were laughing at her. She smiled vaguely.

At the gate next to theirs, boarding had commenced. A long line materialized instantly. A baby began crying, which set off the others around it. The plane was headed to a place that the student wasn't familiar with. The baby's parents had boarded a plane in the country where they lived, and were taking the baby for the first time to the country they were from.

The mother was holding the baby, rocking it and smiling at it, while the father, standing next to her carrying their luggage, looked around him restlessly. The airport contained an extraordinary number of people. Some were browsing the duty-free and gift shops; security personnel and cleaning staff did their rounds. The father was startled to realize that each of these countless people had some purpose or another for being here. The place was full of people traveling somewhere, or working. Nobody simply found themselves here for no particular

A HUNDRED YEARS AND A DAY / *163*

reason. Feeling somehow dazed by this fact, the father failed to keep up with the moving line, and was prompted by the person behind him. The mother moved forward, holding the baby.

The couple were in this airport only to transfer planes. This was the fourth time that they'd taken this route and transferred here. Each time they'd just rushed around the airport, never venturing outside. They showed their passports upon arrival, were looked at intently by the immigration officials, but knew nothing whatsoever about the country.

The baby's crying didn't stop. An elderly woman with beautiful silver hair standing next to them said, "It's okay. Crying is a baby's job." Hearing this, the father thought to himself that at least the baby wasn't aware of its destination, and felt somehow relieved by this.

The silver-haired woman comforting the baby looked out nostalgically at the runway and the sky behind the glass.

The first time she'd flown from this airport was forty years previously. There were now three terminals here, but at that time, there'd only been one. She'd been living abroad for her husband's work then, and had traveled through this airport to go between here and that country once a year. Back then, she wasn't used to flying, and would get nervous each time. Occasionally there'd be news stories about a major crash. Sometimes her husband was so busy with his work that he'd return before her, meaning she'd have to fly alone. As she stood there in line, she'd glare reproachfully at the airplanes taking off.

It was because those beastly things had been created that she had to feel this fear, and go through the unpleasantness of jet lag.

Once, while anxiously checking in her luggage, her father, who'd come to see her off, said to her, flying's no big deal. Twenty-five years before, he had taken off numerous times from here in planes that he himself flew. That had been during the war. It was a cargo aircraft that he flew, not a fighter, and yet each time he took off he'd be haunted by the thought that he might never return. One time he'd encountered an enemy aircraft while he was in the air. It appeared to be a spy plane, and it flew off. Still, he felt all the blood drain from his body. Someone he knew from his hometown had taken off and never returned. They were told that he'd likely crashed into the sea, but they never recovered the fuselage.

The airfield had once been a golf course, an officer who had grown up in the area had told him. He'd said that rich people had come from far and wide to spend the day there. The officer died just before the war ended. Seeing his daughter off at the gleaming white terminal, the father was struck by the thought that his still being alive was some kind of mistake.

The father hadn't been on a plane since the war ended. By some coincidence, he had found a job at a company with a factory near the airfield, married a woman who worked at the same factory, and had three children. During that time, the airfield had become an international airport. The terminal was built, a row of aircraft hangars appeared, and jets incomparably larger than the cargo planes that he had flown took off thunderously.

There were several hundred landings and takeoffs a day. White planes vanished into the sky, and others appeared from the distance.

Far away, beyond that misty sky with its white clouds, lay entirely different places, the student thought. The places to where this unthinkably large number of people would return all existed somewhere off in the distance. It was finally time for them to board. It was the end of both their holiday and their time as students. From next month, a new life would begin for them. The students stood up, picked up their heavy bags bulging with souvenirs, and joined the line.

27

An older sister who's taken a bus to the desert finds that she has phone reception, so sends a photo to her younger sister; her younger sister thinks about the deserts she has visited in the past

It had never occurred to the older sister that you could get to the desert by bus. She'd always believed you needed a specially designed vehicle, like the sturdy cars driven in one of the races that went for days on end across numerous countries, which she'd happened to see one sleepless night when she'd turned on the TV in the early hours. Or else you traveled in a caravan of camels like those she'd seen in picture books depicting tales from the past.

From amid the incessant stream of English on the audio guide, she made out the word "highway." For the older sister, whose English was shaky, the audio guide hovered on the border of comprehensibility, and she had to try and piece together its gist from the few simple words that she could pick up. Highway—a straight road cutting through the desert. A road, and nothing else. No road signs, no lights. For a while after setting out from the town where her hotel was, she'd seen houses dotted here and there, but now, wherever she looked there were only endless expanses of reddish sand with an undulating pattern, like waves.

It was strange to have a road when there were no buildings, the older sister thought. Then she realized that she'd never thought before about which came first: roads or cities. In the place she'd lived until now, roads spanned the spaces between buildings. They crept along the ground, connecting all the space left over from the structures looming on either side. If there were no buildings, it seemed to her, then you could go anywhere—there was no need for roads. Yet, there was a road here. She supposed that without it, the bus would have a hard time traversing the sand.

I'm sitting—on a bus—headed for the desert—right this moment.

The older sister arranged the phrases in a line in her head, as if to make sure of them. The sun slanting through the windows made even the bus's interior very bright, and the older sister put on her sunglasses. She didn't have sunglasses of her own, because she didn't go out very much, so she'd borrowed them from her younger sister, who was fond of traveling. Her younger sister had already visited the desert three times. It was so amazing, it changed my perspective on life, the older sister had heard her younger sister say, but the two didn't live together, and the older sister had set out for the desert without ever asking her sister's impressions of it in more detail.

In the adjacent seat her former colleague, who had planned the trip, was asleep. The older sister felt it was a waste to sleep through this, but her colleague was suffering from jet lag and had been complaining about a lack of sleep, so she held off waking her until they arrived.

She'd only looked away from the window for a moment, while she rooted around in her bag and then glanced at her colleague's face, but when she returned her gaze outside, she was surprised to see several shops, where previously there had only been sand.

A gasoline stand, a diner, a grocery store. All were jerry-built constructions, and although they must have been put up only recently, the coating of sand they wore gave them an aged look. In front of them lay some gateposts, and a big sign in the shape of a camel. The bus passed through the gateposts into a huge parking lot, with space for two hundred cars. A parking lot for desert sightseeing. A little bewildered by how different everything was from how she'd been imagining it, the older sister clambered into the four-wheel-drive vehicle along with her former colleague, who had woken up of her own accord in the end, and was in high spirits. By that time, the sun was setting, and it was beginning to get dark.

The high-octane drive lasted about ten minutes before they arrived at a line of what looked like nomadic tents. They took off their sandals and walked barefoot. The sand beneath their feet still retained its heat. It was easier to walk barefoot than in sandals or shoes. Turning to look behind her, all she could see was sand. Sand dunes went on and on like waves. The camel sign must have been there somewhere, but from this angle it really felt as though she'd arrived at the end of the earth.

There was going to be a dance show under the night sky beginning shortly, she heard from someone. She took out her smartphone, took a square photograph of the sand looking like a mountain range, and sent it to her sister. She had lent her sunglasses, after all. She had phone reception, and there was Wi-Fi she could connect to as well.

The younger sister, who was at home when she received the picture, said, ahh, I wanna be *there*. She held out her phone screen to her husband, who was eating breakfast opposite her. Look, she said.

Oh, wow, he replied, and then, without seeming particularly interested, you've been to the desert before though, right?

I have, the younger sister said. I have, but I want to go again, and it never stops being impressive however many times you go, and besides, every desert is a different color, so it feels different, she went on emphatically.

Though the younger sister didn't know it, houses now stood in the bit of desert where she'd ridden on a camel ten years previously. Owing to the sudden economic development of its neighbor, the country with the desert was experiencing an increase in immigration and people moving there for work, and the government had begun development projects in certain areas. In that spot she'd visited, which had been just sand, roads appeared, and then the surrounding area was divided neatly into blocks and sold off as residential land. About sixty percent of it was now taken up by housing.

But what the younger sister pictured as she sipped coffee from the cup she'd just refilled was a totally different scene. Not long before, she'd seen a TV program about how the desert was expanding. Accompanying the powerful narration, which described how the desert had reached the ocean and was now continuing along the ocean floor, was underwater footage showing white sand and blue sea. That desert was very far west—several thousand kilometers due west from the easternmost point of the continent on which the younger sister was now drinking her coffee. The two places were connected.

The younger sister looked around her, wondering if this place here would also be covered by sand at some point. Would even this small coastal country—where ever more high-rise buildings were being built, and where the sight of soil beneath one's feet had disappeared long ago—be returned to desert someday in the distant future?

I'd be too terrified to go to the desert, her husband said. Why, the younger sister asked. When I was a kid I watched this film where someone's car breaks down in the desert and they end up dying, and I still haven't been able to forget about it, he said, making various gestures that illustrated someone suffering and dying.

The younger sister laughed loudly, then said, you'd be okay now, because you can use phones out there. Look, she just sent another photo.

The younger sister's phone screen displayed the photo just sent by her older sister, of the desert as darkness set in.

28

**One day, there was a great snowfall in a place
where snow never usually settled; a boy who had
run out of his house saw a black dog in a park,
and then immediately afterward heard someone
from his year at school calling his name**

It had started to snow.

The snow that had begun falling in the early hours of
Wednesday was the heaviest ever seen in that region, and
when people awoke in the morning, they found the area
covered in white as far as the eye could see.

The weather forecast the previous day had predicted
only a possible light dusting. Accordingly, neither the
public transportation companies nor the residents were
well prepared. Chaos set in at the airport, and it closed
shortly after. The trains were seriously delayed, and by the
afternoon, the town was more or less cut off.

The snow didn't stop. With the recent change in the
weather patterns, the region now experienced a heat
wave every few years, which brought the place to a standstill, but cold snaps and great snowfalls were utterly
unexpected, and it was the first time many local residents
encountered such a thing.

By the third day, the lake—which took up half the
park in the town's center, and was also the source of the
town's name—began to freeze over. This was unheard of,
even among the adults who'd grown up there. School was

suspended, and the TV repeatedly entreated people not to venture outside, but a few children looked for an opportunity to slip out.

A boy who lived on the fourth floor of an apartment building on a street near the park snuck out while his parents were glued to the TV news and headed directly for the lake. The news wasn't yet reporting that it had frozen over, but the boy knew from overhearing his parents talking on the phone.

The park, usually so full of kids and elderly people taking walks, lay absolutely still. The boy tramped across the deserted square of grass and up the perfectly white hill. Leaving a trail of footprints in the snow was very enjoyable. The snow began to fall harder, and when the boy turned to look behind him, he saw his footprints had already been covered over by fresh snow.

Arriving at the lake, the boy saw a man walking his dog.

It was a big black dog. Making its way through the whiteness with most of its body held perfectly still, it looked like a silhouette. The boy from the fourth floor was amazed that someone would take their dog for a walk in weather like this. The man and the dog came closer, so the boy asked,

"What's its name?"

The name the man pronounced was short and strange sounding. The man explained that it meant "black" in a foreign language. There was snow in the man's hair. The man walked off, as if pulled along by the dog. Even close up, the dog was pure black in color.

Hearing his name being called from afar, the boy turned to see another boy from his year who lived in the building next to his.

I've been looking for you, the other boy said, curtly. Your parents are going crazy because you've disappeared. Won't they be looking for you, too, if you're here, the fourth-floor boy replied, huffily. It's okay, the other boy said, smiling. I said I was going to look for you.

The two walked right up to the edge of the lake. It was frozen solid, and snow had settled on its surface. They debated walking on it, but when he was younger, the boy from the fourth floor's grandpa had told him a story of a boy who'd gone walking on a frozen lake and died when the ice had cracked beneath him, and he was too scared. Instead, he left the park with the boy from the next-door building, and the two of them did a loop of the town.

The town was so dark that it was hard to believe it was the middle of the day. Everything seemed blue, tinged with gray. The sounds of their voices and their feet treading the snow were instantly absorbed by the dark masses of snow and the dim shadows.

It's scary, the boy from the fourth floor said.

It's not scary, it's beautiful, the boy from the next-door building said. Looking at the fallen snow sparkling blue-white at their feet despite the darkness of the sky, from which fresh snow fell ceaselessly, the fourth-floor kid wondered if in fact those two words, scary and beautiful, meant the same thing. At this moment, the town was scary and beautiful, beautiful and scary.

For five days, the snow continued to fall. The

first-floor windows were buried, then ice appeared even on the river, forming sleety clumps where the current was sluggish. A state of emergency was declared, and people were ordered not to go outside. For a time there was concern about food shortages. On the morning of the sixth day, though, the sky cleared, the temperature rose, and the snow began to melt. After a few days, once the trains began running again and food reappeared in the shops, the town returned to normal, as if nothing had happened.

Nothing, except that the boy from the next-door building had gone missing. The boy from the fourth floor who'd walked around outside with him on that day was questioned by the police, but he'd not seen the boy since they'd returned home together, and he'd definitely seen him enter his apartment building. The classmate's parents also testified that the boy had returned to the apartment once that night. By the time they got up the following morning, though, there was no sign of him. A search party was formed to comb the mountains surrounding the town, but with no success. Time passed, with nothing turning up—not his possessions, nor his tracks, nor any clues whatsoever.

After finishing high school the fourth-floor boy worked for two years to save up money, then went to university abroad.

His university was located in a cold town in a cold country. In winter, the snow would shut the place down for five whole months. Looking out at the pure-white scenery every day, the fourth-floor boy would think back

to that winter with the freak snowfall. He'd get the feeling
that his classmate from the next-door building was going
to appear from beyond the dark sky and luminescent
blue-white snow outside his window. It wasn't a scary
feeling. It was closer to a kind of nostalgia.

29

There were several fountains in the underground shopping complex at any one time; a square there known as Fountain Plaza was used by many as a meeting place; several decades previously, several years previously, there had been people waiting for other people there

The square known as Fountain Plaza in the underground shopping complex was used as a meeting place.

There were lots of fountains in that one shopping complex. Every year they seemed to get fancier—there were those whose flow pattern modulated according to the time of day, those that lit up in rainbow colors, and so forth. They'd presumably been put there to take the edge off the confined feeling that shoppers got from being underground.

The underground shopping complex was one of the biggest in the country. It had a convoluted structure, having started out as a number of independent underground shopping centers that grew out of the stations for the various private railway lines that operated there. Then another underground shopping center was built beneath the office buildings in front of the station, and gradually all the underground centers connected up. When you saw a map of the entire thing, it looked like a patchwork sewn together from numerous spider's webs. It was hard even for those who passed through it every day on their commute to grasp it in its entirety.

The place known as Fountain Plaza lay at the east end of the huge underground shopping complex. Above ground in that spot were three cinemas and an area with lots of bars and clubs, which was how the square had become a popular meeting place. Its name was often mentioned on signs giving directions and in TV commercials: "Right by Fountain Plaza!" "Two minutes' walk from Fountain Plaza."

The year that Kazumi Matsuo entered senior high school, there was a bookstore by Fountain Plaza that specialized in manga. Kazumi, who walked through that part of the underground complex twice a day on her way to and from school, would stop into the bookstore about twice a week.

"Found anything good?"

Taken aback by the sound of this voice suddenly addressing her, Kazumi dropped the hardcover book that was in her hands.

"Oh, sorry!"

Standing there was Naoko Nishiyama, a girl in her class. The two girls would say hi when they saw each other, but weren't especially friendly.

Naoko picked up the book from the floor.

"Ah, my sister really likes that series." Unfazed by Kazumi's obvious shock, Naoko went on speaking with a smile. "She's about to publish her first manga."

"Oh, right."

"She's told me not to tell anyone, so don't tell anyone, okay?"

"Okay."

For a while the two of them stood perusing the shelves full of manga, saying, this one's really good, this one was kind of lacking something for me, then they left the store. As ever, there were lots of people standing around the fountains, waiting.

"You know this fountain?" Naoko murmured, as if telling Kazumi a secret. "They say that if you stand here and wait long enough, then a long-haired woman comes and talks to you."

Kazumi ran through in her mind the various plausible reasons why that might be the case, so Naoko's next words caught her by surprise.

"She's a ghost, and you mustn't go off with her when she asks you to."

Kazumi didn't believe in ghosts, and found herself at a loss for what to say. Before she knew it, she was saying,

"I had some old man I didn't know come up and talk to me once, saying he'd give me money if I went off with him."

Sometimes middle-aged men, even men she suspected were close to her grandfather's age, would make obscene comments to her. At that time, on TV and in magazines, people were forever discussing how Japanese society had lost its head over female high school students, but how this manifested in reality was as a kind of contempt. The number of men directing such contemptuous remarks at girls like her was on the rise.

"Yuck. What's with those kind of guys?" Naoko said, pulling an expression of genuine repulsion.

"I want to know what would happen if you did go off with that ghost woman, but I guess there's no way of finding out."

"I feel like a ghost is less scary than someone with bad intentions?"

"Yeah, she probably has her reasons for acting like that, right?"

From that day on, Kazumi and Naoko began speaking to each other more in the classroom. Sometimes they'd make the detour to Fountain Plaza together and talk about manga. Naoko and Kazumi lived in opposite directions from their school, and this underground shopping complex wasn't on Naoko's way, but she could navigate its labyrinthine passages perfectly. She said that she'd learned from her sister, but Kazumi was always astonished by her unerring sense of direction. At some point, the two began going together to one of the above-ground cinemas.

One Saturday, when their third year of school was ending and they were about to graduate, Kazumi was in Fountain Plaza, reading a manga as she waited for Naoko.

"Any good?"

Lifting her head, she saw a long-haired woman standing right beside her. The woman wore the white shirt and navy blazer associated with school uniforms, but she looked like she was in her thirties or possibly forties.

"Er, yeah, it is."

"Can I take a look?"

"Um, yeah, sure."

The woman held the manga right up to her face as if she had very bad eyesight.

Feeling frightened, Kazumi remembered what Naoko had told her on that day she'd spoken to her in the manga shop. But the woman was casually commenting on the manga.

"So, this is what kids these days are into, is it?"

"I'm not sure. People say I have strange taste."

"But it's selling, right?"

"Among certain people. Nobody else at my school understands what's good about it, though."

"Oh, is that right! Wow ..."

The woman finally handed the manga back to Kazumi.

"Where are you off to now?"

"I'm waiting for a friend."

"Now listen, you can't just go along with what other people want you to do, you know? You've got to do what *you* want. That's the only way you'll be satisfied in life. Regardless of how it pans out."

"Ah, right, okay."

As Kazumi stood there, dazed by this piece of unsolicited advice, the woman waved and walked off.

Kazumi waited for close to an hour and finished reading the manga she'd just bought, but Naoko didn't show. She tried calling her from a public payphone, but nobody picked up. She was worried, but there was nothing else for her to do, so she went home and tried calling Naoko again. This time Naoko picked up. When Kazumi asked what had happened, Naoko let out a startled cry, then apologized repeatedly, saying that she'd thought it was tomorrow they were meeting. She'd been at home the whole time, but hadn't heard the phone ring.

After leaving high school, Kazumi went to university in Tokyo. She was the only girl from her school who went on to study in Tokyo. Naoko came to visit several times while they were both students, but when Kazumi took a job in a faraway part of the country, the two saw less of each other.

After leaving the company where she'd worked for fifteen years, Kazumi returned to the city in which she'd grown up. She got in touch with Naoko for the first time in ages, and the two arranged to meet in Fountain Plaza. The area around the station had been redeveloped and looked considerably different. Kazumi had set out early, but after getting lost and consulting several maps, she arrived barely on time, just as a message arrived from Naoko apologizing and saying she was going to be late.

The dynamic sound of the cascading water took her back to the olden days. A senior high school boy stood next to her, absorbed in a manga.

"Is that any good?" Kazumi asked him, before she could stop herself. The boy didn't seem too surprised, and answered in a friendly manner.

"It's not bad."

At that moment, Kazumi realized that she herself looked exactly like the woman who'd spoken to her when she was a high school student, and laughed.

"They're getting rid of this fountain next month, apparently."

"Oh really." It was hard to work out whether he was listening to what she was saying.

"You've got to do the things you like doing. That's the only way you'll be satisfied in life, if you do the things you want."

"Why are you saying that to me, out of the blue?"

"I just felt like saying it, out of the blue."

"Right."

Out of the crowd, Naoko came running toward her. What's going on? she asked, and Kazumi replied, it's a good question.

30

Family Tree III

My grandmother had a younger brother who moved to the big city to find work straight out of junior high school. At first, he worked as a carpenter's apprentice. The carpenter he trained under was strict but looked after those in his care, and the boy was quick to learn. The carpenter's more senior apprentices, though, seized upon any opportunity to beat up the boy. They were sure to do it when the boss wasn't looking. They fed him lies about things at work that led him to make several grave mistakes, and his reputation suffered as a result.

After running away from the carpenter's workshop, he worked various jobs, delivering newspapers, then rice, and working in the warehouse of a transportation company, before he moved to a city at the mouth of a big river and once again began working for a carpenter. This time he wasn't bullied. This was a period when a seemingly endless number of houses were being built, and there were never enough people to build them, so wages were rising. He was treated well by his new boss's family, who often made him dinner.

On his days off, he would go to the grassy stretch beside the river and watch people playing baseball. At some point, he started taking along the old guitar that his boss's son had given him, and strumming it tentatively. He liked it when the sound of the guitar came together with the sound of the wind. After a while, he began making up his own songs. They weren't very good, but if nobody stopped to listen to him, nobody stopped him from playing either. Every Sunday, from lunchtime until evening, he would sit on the riverbank close to the bridge and sing out over the water. They were songs that were only ever sung once.

One Sunday, a man on his way home from playing baseball stopped and listened to my grandmother's brother playing. The following week, the same man came again. He stood a little way off, saying nothing. That went on every Sunday for six months.

The songs that my grandmother's brother played back then are known only to him and that man.

31

**Mako was always watching TV; after seeing
an astronaut on TV she decided to become
an astronaut, and went to the moon**

Mako Kondō would turn on the TV as soon as she got home
from school and watch reruns of dramas and anime, and
then she'd leave it on while the evening news played.
It was the exact same most days. All her friends went to
cram school, but Mako didn't. Instead she watched TV.

Into the summer vacation, the people in her year
would attend what they called "summer courses," and the
amount of time Mako spent alone increased. All of that
became TV time. One day, as she was reading manga with
the news on in the background, she heard the presenter
announce that the first Japanese female astronaut had
gone up in a space shuttle. Flicking her eyes to the screen,
she saw a female astronaut in a blue spacesuit floating in
a white-walled vestibule inside the shuttle, carrying out
some kind of test. At that moment, Mako decided that she
would also become an astronaut, and started studying on
her own.

Even into junior high and then senior high Mako
couldn't go to cram school, so when school finished she'd
go to the library, stopping by the staff room when she
wanted to ask the teachers questions. She asked so many
questions that one teacher remarked to her, "This isn't
a cram school, you know!" Yet Mako continued unfazed,

and became the first person from her school to get into the science department of a national university in the Kantō region.

Mako liked university, because it enabled her to study the things she wanted to her heart's content. Once she started her graduate course and joined the research department, she stayed there late every night. She made sure to factor in time to build up her physical strength and to study the foreign languages needed to become an astronaut. When she returned late to her small dorm room, she would watch TV for the short period until she fell asleep. There were no longer any programs she particularly enjoyed, but switching on the TV was a habit for her, and somehow having it on helped her to fall to sleep. She imagined that it was because, so long as she was watching TV, she wasn't using her brain.

She usually set the TV to switch off automatically at a certain time, but once, when she woke in the middle of the night, it was still on. The screen showed a foreign film where an astronaut was left alone in a spaceship. After much strenuous effort, the astronaut managed to return to earth, but all the people on earth had since died. Plants and animals lived on—had, in fact, grown more abundant now that there were no humans around. The movie ended with a scene where the astronaut looked out at that beautiful scenery and cried. Mako fell asleep before seeing it.

Fifteen years later, a space shuttle took off from a desert somewhere in the Middle East with Mako inside it. The space shuttle, which had five astronauts on board, was carrying humans to the moon for the first time in sixty years. Mako became the first woman to walk on the moon. Looking at Earth from the moon's surface, it struck Mako that it was the same colors as the Earth she'd seen on TV as a child. All the students from Mako's elementary school watched Mako walking on the moon on TV. It was Mako's request that they did so, and she had donated ten TV sets to the school for that purpose.

32

Back when the first train passed through the area, my grandmother's grandfather tended a flock of sheep, and his wife spun their wool; one day, the two finally began talking to each other

Grandpa said that he remembered when the local station had been built and the first train had passed through the region, my grandmother told me. It wasn't my grandfather that she was talking about but hers, which I guess makes him my great-great-grandfather.

The train tracks ran straight through the grassy fields. Apparently there were quite a few people from the town who were sent to help lay the tracks, but my grandmother's grandfather wasn't one of them. He claimed that that was because he was tending to his sheep, but my grandmother said that she didn't know if that meant that he couldn't go because he was too busy with his shepherding work, or that he already had sufficient income, or if he meant something else by it.

He had spoken to my grandmother on numerous occasions, back when she was a child. She had listened to his stories as if they were tales of the olden days out of a picture book. She never thought of his stories as referring, for example, to the station that you could see in the distance from that cottage on the hill where they lived.

The station was a small brick building. Only trains with a couple of cars stopped there, and then only once a day. Longer trains with numerous cars would pass through several times a day without stopping.

Work had begun on the train tracks not long after my grandmother's grandfather had married. He had been given the land on which to tend his sheep by his wife's father, and the sheep themselves by one of his father's relatives. He had fixed up the dilapidated cottage, which had stood abandoned for a long time on top of a hill outside of town, right in the middle of the land he'd been given, to live in. The townspeople said that the stone cottage had once been inhabited by foreigners. The foreigners spoke a different language, and came from the other side of the forest. Then, before anyone knew it, they'd disappeared.

As he was fixing up the cottage, the man would think a lot about the people who built it. The way the stones were laid was definitively different from the other houses in the neighborhood. From inside the ashes in the hearth emerged an iron plate, of a shape he'd not seen before. It had traces of some kind of lettering on it, but he couldn't read them. He couldn't really read very well in general, so he wasn't even sure whether it was his language or not. He saved the plate and put it in the barn, but after a while he forgot where he had left it.

The townspeople went out every day to their appointed spot on the tracks. As the days went on, their number increased. When my grandmother's grandfather was leading his sheep to a different pasture, he would sometimes see the workers from a distance, digging up the earth and carrying sections of steel track. When he ran into them from time to time, they'd complain about the engineers and railway company employees from the city. With lots of new people around, the only bar in town began to do a roaring trade, eventually buying up the building next door so it could extend its premises.

My grandmother's grandfather very rarely went to the town. In the morning he'd take his sheep out to graze, then return to the cottage, tend to the small field by the cottage that produced just enough food for him and his wife to eat, deal with anything that needed doing in the sheep barn, then herd the sheep back. He didn't talk much to his wife. Their marriage had been arranged by their parents, and he had met her only twice before their wedding. He had heard from his wife's relatives, as well as from his own parents, that she didn't talk much. She had been like that since childhood.

His wife helped out in the wool workshop run by the local women, leaving after breakfast and coming back in the evening. She was in charge of dyeing the wool there. It was only after marrying her that he had learned you could use the grasses and berries in the forest, as well as onion skins and carrot leaves and other things, to dye things in pretty colors. The few things that his wife did say were about what substances she had used to dye the small quantities of wool she'd brought home with her, and how successful the dyeing process had been. While she was at home, she would silently knit caps, gloves, and small blankets with the wool she'd brought back.

In contrast with the track-laying work that unfolded gradually, the station building seemed to materialize overnight. One day, when he took the sheep to the hill that

A HUNDRED YEARS AND A DAY / *191*

offered the best view of the station, my grandmother's grandfather noticed a dark square patch that hadn't been there a few days previously.

He had been to the city just once, three years before. He went along to carry the bags for a relative who had a much larger flock of sheep and was visiting a customer who bought his wool. They walked as far as the next town, and there took a horse-drawn cart and then a boat traveling down the river. Arriving in the big city for the first time, he felt as though he'd fallen into a bad dream: the air was full of smoke, and the towering buildings looked as though they might topple on him at any moment. The station in the big city was truly a thing of magnificence. He had never seen a building that palatial outside of a church. The largest building he'd seen up until that point was the cathedral in the city where his parents lived, but that station seemed even more solid and impossible to move.

So he assumed that the station building in the town would be similarly stately, even if it wasn't quite that grand.

When he asked the men living locally who were working on it, they told him that since there weren't many passengers who'd get on and off there, they were essentially constructing a box, sufficient as a place for people to disembark and to board from.

When he went back home, he relayed this information to his wife. She listened in silence and then, after a long pause, told him that she had helped lay the bricks for the station. Surprised, the man asked her when she'd

192 / TOMOKA SHIBASAKI

been doing that. She told him that they'd run out of build-ers, and so the people from the wool workshop had been sent over to help. She told him with a serious face that she was the strongest of all the women in the workshop. When he told her that he'd never known that about her, she pointed out the window to one of the stones heaped by the entrance to the sheep barn, a stone that was larger than all the others, and said, I can lift a stone like that one.

His wife had worked with him to fix up the cottage, he recalled, but he hadn't noticed her strength then. Now that he thought about it, he realized that she'd never seemed tired, despite carrying stones and lumber all day, and he remembered that she'd lifted some pretty heavy-looking things. He'd been convinced that someone so petite couldn't have that kind of strength, though, and hadn't asked her to help with the really heavy lifting.

He felt quite astonished by this revelation, and asked his wife a series of questions. For a while she kept quiet and looked into his face as if assessing him. Then she got to her feet, wrapped her hands around his chest, and lifted him clean off the floor, before gently setting him down again.

For a few moments after it happened he felt a bit dazed, but then he looked at her standing there, as though it was no big deal, and cried out, but that's amazing! I've never met a woman with that kind of strength before! His excited voice echoed round the small cottage interior. At this, his wife finally smiled. She looked genuinely happy. It was the first time that he'd seen a look of such happi-ness on her face.

She brewed some tea, and then began to tell him stories, starting from her childhood. She told him how her parents had been surprised when she'd lifted up pieces of farming machinery, how when she'd gotten older she'd been teased by boys at school so she'd learned to hide her strength, how her wool workshop was full of women, and so lots of people relied on her for her strength. But I knew that if I lifted up the things at the station as if it was easy for me, then I'd be given more work, so even when I was carrying the smallest bricks I pretended that I found them really heavy, she said, with a faintly proud expression. It was the first time for him to experience her speaking like this, too, and it came as a great surprise.

From that point on, the woman began talking to her husband more regularly, even if she wasn't as garrulous as his female relatives. She would talk to him about the completed station building, and do impressions of the unpleasant railway company executives. She'd tell him of her amazement when the wool turned out a beautiful hue, and what forest plants generated what shades. The time he spent talking with her was a time of great happiness for him.

A month after the station opened, the first train passed through. All the townspeople came and stood in a great crowd to see it. The man and woman watched it from the top of the hill, where they could see the track in its entirety.

The first thing they saw was the smoke—a patch of gray-black drifting from beyond the forest. After a while, a mass of glinting black metal appeared. They could feel the ground rumbling beneath them, far off as they were. It seemed to them as though the forest and plains they'd been looking at all this time had been painted over in another color. The sheep that were grazing near the tracks, sheep that had formerly been white with black faces, were now black all over.

My grandmother never met her super-strong grandmother. She had died when my grandmother's father was still a young child. The only photo of her that existed was hanging in the cottage that my grandmother had lived in growing up.

The woman in the photo was shorter than my grandmother's grandfather. She stood next to him and had slender shoulders. It was impossible to imagine her having the kind of strength that my grandmother's grandfather had made her out to have. Yet with one arm she was holding her three-year-old son—my grandmother's father—with as much ease as if he were a teddy bear.

My grandmother had visited the stone cottage where they'd lived just once when she was a child. Her father had taken her, after his own father had died, to collect his personal effects. The central part of the town had changed since the station was built, and no one lived along the path to the cottage. Her grandfather had sold his sheep a few years earlier but had remained in the cottage until his death. My grandmother, who had grown up in a town that was lively even if it was remote and rural, was amazed by how bare the cottage was. They had gone to collect her grandfather's possessions, but they found only a few pieces of furniture and cutlery there.

My grandmother went there once more, several decades later. While visiting a nearby town to attend a relative's funeral, she'd had the idea of walking the path she remembered to the hill where the cottage had been.

In her memory, the hill wasn't that far from the station, but in fact it was quite a distance. There was no building on the hill where the cottage had once been. There was a pile of stones of a similar sort of size, though, and seeing them, my grandmother understood that they had once been the cottage. She picked up a few of the stones, but she couldn't find any bearing marks that would indicate in which part of the former cottage they had been laid.

Some years ago they were thinking about tearing down the local station, which had fallen into disuse with the depopulation of the area, but then people made the case for it being of historical value, and one part of it was preserved and made into a small museum. I'm planning to visit this museum next summer. It'll be the first time for me to visit the country where my grandmother grew up. As far as I can tell from photographs, the preserved part of the station is still there, just as it was when it was first built.

33

**On the first floor of a building were several
small shops; a woman who opened a cafe at
the back of the building was told by a fortune
teller that a bright future awaited her**

The corridor passed through the old building that had no
elevator and led out onto the alley behind. The corridor
was dingy, with little shops packed tightly along either
side, and you couldn't tell from glancing at the building's
facade that it led all the way out to the back. But the people who frequented this part of town, which was teeming with second-hand clothing shops, record shops, and
bars, knew this passageway and the shops lining it. Each
shop was only the size of a single room in an apartment.
When the building was first completed, they were offices.
The first shop you came to was a hat shop, then a record
shop, opposite that was a vintage shop. Next to the vintage shop was another vintage shop, then a place selling
imported mugs, then there was another second-hand
clothing shop, and then right at the back, a cafe.

Or rather, it declared itself a cafe, but it had only a single, largish table. With four people inside, it became impossible for anyone to move around the space. The tall woman
at the little counter stooped as she prepared the coffee. The
only things on the menu were coffee and buttered toast.

At times, customers from the hat shop and vintage
shops would come in, and others, people living in the

apartments at the end of the alleyway, stopped by. It was in such an out-of-the-way location that when it first opened, the only customers were people that the owner knew and their acquaintances.

Because it was positioned at the very back of the building, the cafe had a window that looked out onto the alley behind. The alley was hemmed in by apartment blocks and mixed-use buildings, but in the space just in front of the window, it opened out a little. A rusty bench had been there since goodness knows when, and sometimes the owner would see people from nearby shops out there smoking.

The person who came most regularly to smoke there was the man from the hat shop. The hat man was saving up money to become a hat-maker. Selling hats didn't earn him enough to save, so he worked evenings at a nearby bar. Once, the hat man brought one of his customers from the bar to the cafe. The customer was a woman, and it was hard to tell if she was young or old. She wore black clothes that trailed along the floor.

"Your coffee is so good," she said. She had a Kansai accent.

"Right? I always say that she must be putting some secret powder in there or something!"

Ignoring the hat man's joke, the customer said to the cafe owner, "You're going to make it big one day. I can see the future, you see."

"Oh yeah? People often tell me that." The woman from the cafe was used to customers saying those kinds of things, so she smiled back at the woman.

"I'm not joking. I can see an amazing light behind you. It's the first time I've ever seen it this strongly. You're our witness," she said, turning now to the hat man. "When this woman becomes famous in the future, I want you to say, what that woman said came true! Okay?"

"Say to who?"

"To anyone . . . I'm not asking for money or anything. I just like seeing the amazing aspects of amazing people."

Nodding in satisfaction at these enigmatic words of hers, she drained her coffee and left a 10,000-yen note on the table. The hat man and the cafe woman used the money to take the people from the record shop and second-hand clothing shops for yakiniku.

The shop next to the cafe that had formerly been a vintage shop became a candle shop, the record shop became a sneaker shop, and the hat man went to study under an Italian milliner. The cafe remained a cafe. When the candle shop moved, the cafe owner began renting that space too, so that you could come and go between the two premises. There were now three tables, and tropical juice and cheesecake were added to the menu. The building next door had been made into a glass-fronted mixed-use building that leased out offices and retail spaces, and there were more young people living in the apartment block at the end who nobody knew anything about, but the little rest area in the alley that you could see from the cafe window remained mostly unaltered. People came to smoke there, and couples sitting there would get into arguments, but most of the time, there was just a bench with nobody on it.

Just before the sneaker shop closed down, an actor known for his sneaker obsession came to the shop in search of some kind of rare find, and stopped in at the cafe on his way home. The actor had been born nearby, and said that he had often hung around the neighborhood when he was young.

"Come to think of it, I bought a hat here too. From a very enthusiastic guy."

"Right! He's gone to Italy, and I've not heard from him since, but I'm guessing he's become a milliner."

In the actor's next movie, he suggested to the director that they use the corridor for one of the locations. The movie, which featured some foreign actors as well as Japanese ones, was only a small production but it received an award at an overseas film festival, and fans from both Japan and overseas began occasionally visiting the cafe. The menu was as limited as ever: just coffee, tropical juice, buttered toast, and cheesecake.

By the time the number of people who remembered the movie was tapering off, it was announced that the old building with its corridor through to the alley behind was to be demolished. There was a problem with its capacity to resist earthquakes, the real estate agent who came to issue the eviction request explained. The cafe moved to a site ten minutes' walk away. The owner placed the same table in the new place, and kept the same menu.

After five years, the owner was scrolling through articles online when she stumbled on one about an esteemed millinery boutique in Tokyo, and realized it was the new venture of the man who had previously owned the hat

200 / TOMOKA SHIBASAKI

shop. The man was saying that he only accepted a limited number of orders, and made them all himself from start to finish.

She didn't know if this quite classified as "making it big" or not, but it struck her that the person who'd come to the cafe had gotten her and the man from the hat shop mixed up. Maybe she just went around saying stuff like that here, there, and everywhere. It wasn't as if the owner had taken what the woman had said literally, but she did feel as though, thanks to those words, she'd come this far thinking that things would pan out okay for her. When she'd opened the cafe at the back of the building, she'd certainly never imagined it would last this long.

For the first time in a while, the cafe owner went back to the place where her cafe was originally located. An apartment building stood there now, and she assumed that she wouldn't be able to get through to the back alley, but entering the building, she noticed a passageway beside the super's office wide enough for a single person to pass. Walking through, she found herself confronted by a scene that she recognized.

Quite unexpectedly, the back of the apartment building was much brighter than it had once been. The building that had been used as storage for a wholesaler was gone, and in its place there was a small two-story red-brick building. Its first and second floors were home to different restaurants. They looked like stylish, expensive establishments. Where the rusty bench had been, a line of tropical plants stood in large terracotta pots.

I'm not joking. I can see an amazing light behind you. The voice of the fortuneteller came back to her suddenly with great clarity. Looking up, she saw a small section of blue sky bordered by the straight lines of the high buildings.

It looked exactly the same as the sky she'd seen every day when she'd been working there.

34

At the back of a building that was being demolished was an apartment that hadn't been touched for decades, containing a manuscript that someone had left behind; a man from the demolition company tried to sell the manuscript but couldn't get any money for it

It was only when a buyer had finally been found, and someone from the demolition company went to carry out a preliminary survey of the building, that they discovered the apartment.

Because the building's owner had changed several times over the years, it was impossible to ascertain whether the family who had lived for many years on the top floor knew of the apartment's existence or not. After they'd given up the four-story brick house, it had been handed over to a real estate company who intended to sell it on, and then lay abandoned for over ten years during the recession.

When the two men from the demolition company opened the gray door at the end of the second-floor corridor, something flapped and flew at them, and they stepped back in surprise. Looking around, though, they couldn't see anything.

The apartment was hemmed in by buildings on both sides, with a building close behind as well, and though it had windows, it felt dingy. It wasn't large, just a living room with a kitchen and one other room. There was a faint smell of moldy boards, but the room itself was clean. It had been well kept. On the table sat an empty mug, as though someone had been living there until that very morning.

Also on the table was a sheaf of paper, covered with blue-ink handwriting. It didn't look old—it looked, in fact, as though it had been written quite recently—but when they consulted the date, they saw it had been written over fifty years ago.

In the other room was just a bed. The blanket was folded back as if someone had just gotten up. There was a layer of dust over everything.

The men from the demolition company got in touch with the building's owner, but the owner didn't welcome the call, telling them impatiently to hurry up with the demolition. Their plans for constructing a new building spanning that and the next-door plots of land were already well underway.

One of the men from the demolition company took the sheaf of paper to a used bookstore. He'd seen on the news once that the handwritten manuscript of a famous author had been found in an old house due for demolition and had fetched a high price, so he expected that it might be worth something. The person in the bookstore responded curtly that it was trash, suggesting that the apartment must have been home to a student who was an aspiring novelist.

As it happened, though, the person living in the apartment forty years ago was not the person who'd written the manuscript. The apartment's final inhabitant had been the younger daughter of the family who'd owned the building at the time.

Until entering university, the younger daughter had lived with her family on the fourth floor. Growing up, she had often been told by her family and relatives that she was a bit of an oddball. Whenever she had a spare moment, she'd spend it reading books, or drawing pictures of rocks and beetles. When she was eight, a new tenant came to live on the second floor. The new tenant was a young woman, and it was a while before the girl discovered that the woman was a biology teacher at the junior high school. When the woman saw the girl reading or drawing in the entrance hall or on the stairs, she would always take an interest in what she was doing, and ask her questions. What are you reading? What do you like about it? Do you like those kinds of insects? What do you like about them? In time, the woman began to lend the girl books. Once she gave her an illustrated guide to minerals with beautiful pictures, saying she'd found it in a second-hand bookshop.

The girl read and drew more and more, becoming an avid student. When she announced that she wanted to go to university to study mineralogy, her parents opposed her decision. It would be better for her to enter a reliable company in an administrative role and find a good man to marry, like her older sister had done. Getting a qualification that would enable her to enter a reputable company was understandable, but it was clear to them that becoming knowledgeable about rocks would only cause her problems in the long run. It was the tenant who

A HUNDRED YEARS AND A DAY / *205*

searched out a university and teacher that would suit the girl, and helped her persuade her parents. The parents gave in, and said that the girl could take the entrance exams for university if she was prepared to pay her tuition fees herself.

The tenant also sent the girl several well-paid openings for a home tutor. Then she told her that she was getting married to another teacher in her school and would be moving away. She was considerably above the usual marrying age, but the woman told the girl that she'd finally found someone who she could talk with about her feelings—her true feelings. With this, she handed the girl a sheaf of paper. I wrote all this down so that I wouldn't forget it, but then I realized I wouldn't ever forget it anyway, so I didn't need to write any more. You can read it if you like, or just throw it away, she said, and left. Telling her parents she wanted to concentrate on her studies, the girl moved into the apartment the teacher had vacated.

The woman who wrote the manuscript had started living in the apartment a few years after the war had ended. Evacuating her country of origin during the war and going to live with relatives abroad, she had been relieved to discover when she returned that her hometown hadn't been bombed in the air raids. The next town along, which she saw from the window of the train on her journey home, lay in ruins. Now you could see its church spire from a distance, which you hadn't previously been able to see, and mounds of rubble were still piled up by the train tracks.

The apartment she was shown didn't get much

light, but it was plenty spacious, and most importantly, the family who owned it somehow thought of one of the tenant's female relatives as their benefactor, so they offered to rent it out to her at a very reasonable rate. She worked for a spell at one of the shops in the town, but after a while, she secured a teaching post at a local junior high school. When things finally began to settle down a bit, she began writing down her memories. She wrote about the time back in the beginning when nobody had really understood what was going on, about how daily life had started to become more challenging, and people began scrutinizing their neighbors' behavior, about the first time that planes carrying bombs flew over her head, and then about a childhood friend of hers who had died .... She wrote little by little after getting home from work, on days when she wasn't too tired. Her intention had just been to get it all down on paper, but as she was writing, all kinds of little details would come to her, so that she'd find herself choked with emotion. Waves of sadness overwhelmed her, making it impossible to carry on writing. Talking to the younger daughter of her landlord's family about things totally unrelated to her past allowed some respite. Seeing the girl's eyes brighten whenever she learned something new, she would start to think that maybe she, too, was still capable of something.

Before the war, a man with a bad leg had lived in the apartment. All the other inhabitants in the building remembered the sound of him slowly climbing the stairs and walking down the corridor, dragging his right foot. The man was still young. He worked in the accounts department of an imported goods company near the station. Nobody knew it, but his hobby was making models. He created scenes of little street corners inside small boxes. He would fashion the buildings, paint the tiny lights into their windows, and then create the nightscapes that served as backgrounds. When the war began, his bad leg prevented him from becoming a soldier, but still, it became hard to stay on in his place of work, so he'd returned to the countryside where his mother lived by herself.

The demolition of the building proceeded smoothly, and in two weeks all that remained was an empty lot. The man from the demolition company threw the manuscript that the used bookstore hadn't taken into a trash can on his way home.

About the Author and Translator

TOMOKA SHIBASAKI is an award-winning novelist, short story writer, and essayist. Her books include *Awake or Asleep*, *Viridian*, and *In the City Where I Wasn't*. She won the Akutagawa Prize in 2014 with *Spring Garden*, which has been translated by Polly Barton. In 2016 she participated in the International Writing Program at the University of Iowa. Two of her works have been made into films, including *Asako I & II* (2018), directed by Ryūsuke Hamaguchi.

POLLY BARTON is a literary translator and writer, based in the UK. Recent translations include *Butter* by Asako Yuzuki, *Mild Vertigo* by Mieko Kanai, *Where the Wild Ladies Are* by Aoko Matsuda, *There's No Such Thing as an Easy Job* by Kikuko Tsumura, and *So We Look to the Sky* by Misumi Kubo. In 2021 she published *Fifty Sounds*, a personal dictionary of the Japanese language.